AF669259

A HISTORY *of* OBJECTS

A HISTORY *of* OBJECTS

a collection of stories

carlo pizzati

HarperCollins *Publishers* India

First published in India by HarperCollins *Publishers* 2022
Building No 10, Tower A, 4th Floor, DLF Cyber City, Phase II,
Gurugram – 122002
www.harpercollins.co.in

2 4 6 8 10 9 7 5 3 1

Copyright © Carlo Pizzati 2022

P-ISBN: 978-93-5489-246-2
E-ISBN: 978-93-5489-550-0

This is a work of fiction and all characters and incidents described in this book are the product of the author's imagination. Any resemblance to actual persons, living or dead, is entirely coincidental.

Carlo Pizzati asserts the moral right
to be identified as the author of this work.

For sale in the Indian subcontinent only.

All rights reserved. No part of this publication may be reproduced, stored in a retrieval system, or transmitted, in any form or by any means, electronic, mechanical, photocopying, recording or otherwise, without the prior permission of the publishers.

Cover design by Devangana Dash
Author photo by Tishani Doshi

Typeset in 11/14 Bell MT at
Manipal Technologies Limited, Manipal

Printed and bound at
Thomson Press (India) Ltd

HarperCollinsIn

MIX
Paper
FSC FSC® C010615

This book is produced from independently certified FSC® paper
to ensure responsible forest management.

'Everything in the world exists to end up as a book.'

– Stéphane Mallarmé

Contents

0%

The Hard Drive

All my friends, family and acquaintances hate that I'm almost always right. Why blame me for it? It could be because of my intuition, or deductive skills. Who knows? It just so happens that, in most cases, I'm right.

What does it mean that 'I'm right'? That. I. Am. Right. Trust me. Why waste energy contradicting me? It would be so much simpler if you just accepted this and didn't force me to argue with you, pushing me to convince you with well-articulated facts.

I could do it. And I will do it, if you insist. But why should you resist this truth? If you don't accept this, I'll be forced to wipe away your doubts and then you, like my friends and family, will also start hating the fact that I'm almost always right.

I think people sometimes doubt this undisputable fact simply because there are a few oddities about me. Or what they perceive as oddities. For example, I have a habit of checking how much cash I have in my pocket. Never less than 200 of any currency. But who uses cash anymore, right? Well, I do. I need it. I also often jangle the coins in my pocket. I'm aware of this. Doesn't bother me, why should it bother you? I always need to have a pen with me in case

I need to write down a thought I could later forget. I often check if my house keys are in my pocket. Never in the left pocket, always in the right, next to my banknotes, coins and credit cards organized in a tiny transparent wallet. Money in the right, nothing in the left. And I don't mean anything political by that. Do I?

I also know that I often squeeze my nose and blow to pop my ears. It gives me relief, and I think it helps me hear better. I also think about everything I see, and I often describe it to myself silently, as if I were writing it down. It's part of my stream of consciousness. But that's my job. I'm a writer. I describe, I write. I still print everything out to edit later by hand because I no longer trust computers. Please remember what I told you in the beginning. Remember it? Yes. Correct. I'm almost always right. Do not dismiss what I'm about to tell you. I'm speaking from experience.

Computers, those are things you should not trust. In fact, I most certainly don't trust them. It's not one of those ridiculous 'artificial intelligence/end of the world as we know it' paranoias. I was betrayed by one of them. Android, Linux, iOS? Which brand? Why do you ask? Does it matter? They may act differently, but they're all the same.

They contain everything: a lifetime in photographs and music, which means the soundtrack of all your heartaches, hopes and despairs; your journals; your confessions in the form of emails and chats; and all the details about your money. Not just your memories but also your present and your future.

Even so, I spend most of my time with a computer. I mean, I'm writing on one right now. It's brand new. The previous one left me, breaking down just as I was finally about to write the truth. I had accumulated hundreds of pages for my book – memories, notes, observations – all well organized in the hard drive, a thing that has become so important to me it's as if it's a brother, a wife, an uncle, or someone else who might change my life. A true friend. A confidant.

Okay, yes, it was my fault. I should've backed up my files. But I hadn't yet. Fear of plagiarism, unfounded worries, call it what you will. I just didn't want to put this specific book, which would finally explain everything, out there in the cloud. I was waiting to print out everything first. But then I was betrayed by this electronic fainting that black-holed three decades of my life and work.

The lab called to ask me what I wanted to do. Throw away the entire laptop or erase the hard drive and replace it with a new one? How could they ask a question like this so abruptly, without preparing the owner for the horror that's coming? I squeezed my nose and blew ten times in ten seconds, while I was being told of this loss. Then I had to jiggle my coins for a while, before answering. The hard drive … even the name seems to mock me, like a drive on a road full of waterlogged potholes after a rough storm.

Now, barely ten minutes since I made my decision – I'm rising to the challenge. I will reconstruct everything. I will rewrite my book as I remember it.

Did I tell you I was born in Geneva but raised in Italy? I'm told I'm organized as a Swiss but with the heart of an Italian. And that it would be worse if it were the other way around. So, I will re-organize. First, I must recall the names of the files and then refill them with everything I can remember. I will write the descriptions of the photos, list all the songs I liked, rewrite my notes, my entire book. From scratch.

I had a most important folder called 'FICTION', in all caps because it was – and is – so important to me. I had unfinished manuscripts in it, short stories, some in collections, some still roaming free. Another most important file was called 'IMAGO', filled with videos and photos. I see some of them in my mind's eye, flying past, as in an album you thumb through. I'm trying to remember which videos I had saved, as if I'm creating a collection of memories that never existed. I can't trust what I'm imagining now. A woman, a child, trees, my mother when she was sixteen in a black-and-white picture, me at twenty-one on a beach somewhere on the Gulf of Mexico, a friend reciting something I had written, snowy hills viewed from the windows of a train, a viola playing in the background as a dramatic soundtrack.

I'm not sure all this was really in my hard drive. Not this way. This feels new. Something born in my head. What was my book about? A father, a son, a journey, a betrayal, a discovery. But what were the characters like? Lovable? Not at all. Hateful? Rather. Understandable? Perhaps. What did they want? What did they like? They all reveal themselves to me as puppets, as masks I had created to tell you something that I was too embarrassed to tell you directly.

I created this fairy-tale world with invented names where we could pretend that I was not talking about you and me, but about them, the characters. Use them at leisure; see if you want to be like this one, or feel you are exactly like that one. No need to be embarrassed by truthfulness.

So puerile and weak, though, isn't it? Not my book lost in my lost hard drive, I mean the entire game we are supposed to be playing here. Creating characters to hide our truths.

Why is it so hard to tell you the real story? I'm embarrassed, for one. I know I said it three times already. Mostly, I'm afraid of spoiling the fiction that our lives really are. When we judge the person in front of us, aren't we creating a fictional character?

I distinctly remember one picture lost in the hard drive. It's of me, sitting cross-legged. I'm six years old, wearing only baggy white underwear. My father, behind me, is sitting in the same position, also in hip-hugging briefs. An early morning sun illuminates us, filtering through the windows of our house. He will yell at me later. But was this real, or are they characters I invented?

Now I see a young Swedish friend with dirty blond hair and crazy blue eyes sneering at me. He will betray me and sleep with my girlfriend.

I see an elderly Filipino lady dancing in her mansion in a Latin American town. She is singing. She is making me happy. I love her.

I see a French girl, lithe, jumpy, cursed by the ghost of a dead father. She wants to love me but cannot.

I see a blond woman grabbing me by the left wrist in the woods of Umbria and making me spin, like a child. I laugh.

This is not making sense; my files are jumbled. I cannot reconstruct them. They are gone. That me is gone. How could I have let that happen?

I remember a file with the word 'Objects' in the title. What did it contain? Stories. Histories. A man thinks a coconut scraper is a work of art; a boy wonders if he has a deadly disease; a dead man with a broken finger tries to play the guitar; a husband changes diapers, and his life; a drunk orphan is worried about her online date; a strange boy runs away from home with his cat; a girl gets a new nickname and loses her mind to LSD; a coward decides to change his life when he sees his painted portrait; an uncle hides a gun, which his nephew could find; a gesture of kindness leads to a politically correct fight; a mother fattens her adult son with sweets; a couple cannot escape their own social media fame; a woman cannot have sex and decides to try flying instead; the purchase of an ugly sculpture puts a dent in a relationship; a boy tries to explain his emotions with a new digital invention; a cockroach causes two people to sleep together; a pair of shoes left in a hallway make a mother cry; someone who wants to end his life discovers all he wanted was to be useful; an umbrella is at the heart of a tragedy.

I begin to remember … It's not truly clear … I was working on my computer. It was late at night. I was sleepy, a glass of white wine next to me. I'm beginning to see this memory more sharply now. Am I imagining it, like the others, or remembering it? Not sure. I am looking at my desktop screen with all the neatly organized folders labelled NON-FICTION, HEALTH, TRAVELS, PROJECTS IN PROGRESS, TEXTS, ARCHIVE and TO READ. I'm feeling very tired in this memory, as I look at all this. I take the glass of wine and pour it over the keyboard, feeling the immediate shrill of terror, yet a deep sigh of relief. I'm free, I think. Only by erasing the old me can I build the new one. This is the pompous thought that comes to mind, as I watch the screen blank out, and darken. I stare into it and see only my reflection. My face, my puffy, messy hair and round-rimmed glasses, a sweater wrapped around my shoulders, a T-shirt with the name of a college printed on the chest. Drawn cheeks, corners of the mouth downturned, as if I were tired of continuing to smile. My job now is to describe this person, to reconstruct him and, to begin, what I can tell you is that all his friends, his family and his acquaintances hate the fact that he's almost always right.

The Coconut Scraper

THE ARTIST, WHO ASKED TO BE CALLED CHARLES THE ARTIST, arrived at the house on time. The place was so remote that sometimes taxi drivers refused to manoeuvre their car more than twenty metres along the dirt track that cut across a few fields, and arrived at a light-salmon-coloured house on the Bay of Bengal. When they said no, the husband had to drive out beyond the property gates to collect guests in a red SUV.

But Charles the Artist's chauffeur was no wimp. He'd seen a lot worse. Charles the Artist had another name, a much more common Tamil–Brahmin name, which served him perfectly while he was working in the family business as a top marketing executive, selling, buying, schmoozing, the whole normal thing his brothers and cousins were accustomed to.

Then came the day of the tsunami when Charles the Artist, who was not yet Charles the Artist, was swimming in the ocean. Which is why he didn't realize a tsunami was coming. He was in the water and did not notice the sea retreating from the shore and coming back with a vengeance. Before he knew it, he was propelled at full speed towards the coastline.

When he woke up, he was surrounded by green light. He had been stripped of his bathing suit and felt the burning sensation of bleeding wounds on his shins and had the impression of lying naked in a hammock. Was he dead? Or was he dying? It didn't feel like death. Although how would he know? A year before, when he was about to be fully sedated for a colonoscopy, he had contemplated the idea of death and found, surprisingly, that he was not scared.

Because he felt pain and weakness, he couldn't be dead, he thought. And when he finally gathered strength enough to wave away a long green leaf covering his eyes, he realized he was nestled, barely, at the top of a very tall palm tree.

He managed to climb down slowly, carefully, and walk to the East Coast Road, where he tried to wave down a car. No one would stop. Perhaps no one realized he was a victim of the tsunami, believing instead that he was just a naked, mud-caked bleeding man trying to hitch a ride. Finally, an auto rickshaw driver took pity.

'Please, take me to Fisherman's Cove Hotel. I'm staying there. My money is there, in my room … Please…'

When they arrived, no one would let him in. The security guards tried to shoo away the annoying, mad beggar until, screaming at the top of his lungs, using his best English diction, he convinced them to let him call his driver in Chennai.

The driver was home and was so shocked when he heard the voice as his half-eaten idli fell from his hands.

'We all thought you were dead, Sir!'

'Come get me at Fisherman's Cove. Right away. Get in the car, now!'

The chauffeur obeyed, not thinking he should first call the family of Charles the Artist, who was not called Charles the Artist at that time. He assumed the family had already been called. But they had not. Charles the Artist was in shock and when allowed to make only one call by the concierge, he rang the person he knew would come to his immediate rescue.

Four hours later, Charles the Artist walked straight into his own wake, which was being held at his house. His wife fainted when she saw him. His mother cried and hugged him tightly, then suddenly pulled back, realizing his bleeding wounds were ruining her sari.

Life had to get back to normal. Only, it didn't. Something had snapped. He couldn't put up with the day-to-day of work, shaking hands, grinning at strangers to get contracts signed, rounds of golf, lunch at the Cricket Club, the occasional expensive vacation. The big wave had washed that life away. He needed something more meaningful. He had not imagined death, but he had come close to it. He needed to explain the brilliance with which he now saw life. His new life.

This is why he reinvented himself as a conceptual artist and, within two years, became one of the best-known artists in Tamil Nadu. He became Charles the Artist.

He was visiting the house by the beach to discuss a commission. He was being asked to paint a portrait of the contemporary Indian dance diva who lived there, and while she made herself a gin and tonic, he was being entertained by her husband, the Turkish novelist Olrak Izzatip. A tall man of indistinct middle-age, merely hinted at by his salt-and-pepper hair and by his body, which held on to its athletic form, Olrak was moderately successful in his own country but now languished in the shadow of his much more famous wife.

Charles the Artist sat on a chair against a wall, his back to the sea. Not that he was afraid of the sea. He just would rather not look at it when talking business.

'You know what that is, right, Charles?' Olrak said, with his light Mediterranean accent. He pointed to a metal object on a small table next to Charles's elbow.

'Yes, it's a … coconut scraper, of course.' Charles the Artist smiled. 'Why do you ask?'

'Well, it is, but actually it isn't. It's a work of art. A rare and valuable one...'

Charles the Artist laughed. 'You're joking. This is a coconut scraper; it's used to grate coconut pulp to make chutney. Come on. It's also an old rusty one, can't do much with it now! Look, here … this is the base where you hold it with your feet; this is the stand that ends in this sharp-edged round head, which kind of looks like a sun, doesn't it, with very sharp and short rays?'

'Look again, carefully,' Olrak insisted.

Charles fixed his gaze on the metallic object. An image flashed in his mind. A beach. A cobra in the sand, which turns out to be only a twisted wooden stick.

Olrak was persistent: 'Can you see the silhouette? That the stand looks like a long, flowing cape of a man walking against the wind?'

'Hmm … okay, maybe, I see what you mean, possibly, yes,' Charles the Artist said, not quite convinced but trying to go along with it. The object looked just like a very regular coconut scraper, identical to the one used by the cook in the house he had grown up in, from the time before he was called Charles the Artist.

'Do you see that the head, which you said looks like a star, is actually a representation of a halo ...? This isn't a coconut scraper at all, it's the representation of a saint, and a specific one.'

'Really?' Charles the Artist said with barely concealed incredulity.

'Don't you know the story of the Wandering Saint of Odiyur Lake?'

'The Odiyur...?'

'Don't you know that the name of the little fishermen's village you crossed before arriving here is "Odiyur"?'

'Hmm. I didn't know that, but...'

'Well, would you like to hear the story of the Wandering Saint of Odiyur Lake, the way I heard it from KG Balakrishna, the conceptual artist who sold this piece to me?'

'Balakrishna? KG? Who?' Charles the Artist began to feel uneasy at the thought of another Tamil artist, a conceptual one at that, who would deserve so much attention, and whom they would be talking about instead of his own work.

'Yes, KG Balakrishna. Don't tell me you haven't heard of him?'

'I confess, I haven't. I'm sorry. But do tell the story, please.'

Olrak paused, took a breath, and then began:

'KG Balakrishna told me about a Danish priest who came to Tranquebar, which, at the time – in seventeen-seventeen – was called Tharangambadi, the Village of the Singing Waves, for echoing the sound of the waves crashing against the rocks below the fortress. It was a Danish Christian outpost, and some say it's where the printing press was introduced to India. To print Bibles, of course. And, in fact, the Wandering Saint, who at the time had not yet become the Wandering Saint of Odiyur Lake, had already arrived in south India to preach the Gospels. The locals nicknamed him Saint Coconut Scraper, because he preached with such fervour, aiming to replace their beliefs in their own gods with the insistence of a cook scraping out every last white fibre from the coconut shell.

'Unfortunately, the Wandering Saint had become too insistent. Once, after travelling a few days north, surviving malaria and hostile territories, he found himself near a lake, surrounded by a group of people who asked him to deny his one and only God and to stop trying to convince them to worship a man who'd been nailed onto two sticks. What kind of a god was that? A bleeding, victimized god of suffering, which they had enough of. Suffering, that is … Gods, they told him, were all-powerful. Or should be. And to say that a god could be killed by a mortal was simply illogical and a sacrilege, wasn't it? But the saint argued with them – 'such heresy!' he said. Enraged, the crowd felt they had no other choice but to disgorge him with a coconut scraper. The simplest way to do this was to remove his head altogether and scoop his brains out—'

'*What?*'

'They took his body – and the coconut scraper – and threw them in the lake, right over there, beyond the Buckingham Canal. But a day later, the waters retreated, just as the ocean pulls back before a tsunami, revealing the body of the beheaded saint and the scraper next to it. Hence the legend that his god, the one on the sticks, had performed a miracle to uncover the crime. Word of the miracle spread, causing villagers – for many miles around – to repent immediately and convert to Christianity.'

'Wow!'

'Yes … And even now, during monsoon season, when at night the rain is so loud against tiled and thatched roofs, the villagers swear they sometimes see the long cape of the Saint of Odiyur Lake walking against the wind, his throat slit wide, and a halo glowing over his nearly detached head.'

'But what does KG Balakrishna have to do with it?' said Charles the Artist, now completely wide-eyed and sitting intently forward, no longer leaning back against the wall.

'Well, KG Balakrishna found the original coconut scraper, which the villagers had kept as a relic for centuries in a little chapel on the other side of the lake. He bought it from them and transformed it into a work of art. It's a sort of ready-made, normal, everyday object, an antique perhaps but a piece that becomes a work of art because of the story it contains.'

'Well,' Charles the Artist said, now leaning back again. 'I'll be damned … I never … And I know so many of the myths from this coast. You know, I was washed up on a palm tree not too far from here…'

'Yes,' Olrak said, with a hint of a smile. 'I know, I know.'

'But this…' Charles the Artist said, unable to take his eyes off the coconut scraper. When he did, he noticed that Olrak was now smirking, and looking at his wife, standing in the living room, with a disappointed look on her face, sipping her gin and tonic.

'See, what did I tell you?' Olrak said, breaking out in laughter.

'What? What? It's not true?' Charles the Artist screamed. Then he looked sad. 'Come on, did you just make that up, that whole thing? You didn't. Tell me you didn't, please…'

'No, not the whole thing,' Olrak's wife said. 'I just lost a bet.'

'Wait … and KG Balakrishna?'

'KG Balakrishna or … KGB?' Olrak said. 'The KGB has always been great at making stuff up. My point is that conceptual art is all about the story, and this is a story inside a story. Does it matter if it's true? Can we be sure it isn't? Does it matter if this really happened or not? Isn't it the idea that counts? The fact is that a coconut scraper, this coconut scraper, makes us think of a man wearing a cape walking against the wind. The story holds. That's what counts, at least to me.'

So, Charles the Artist bought the coconut scraper from Olrak for a ridiculously expensive sum and sold it again two months later in Delhi for 250 times that price.

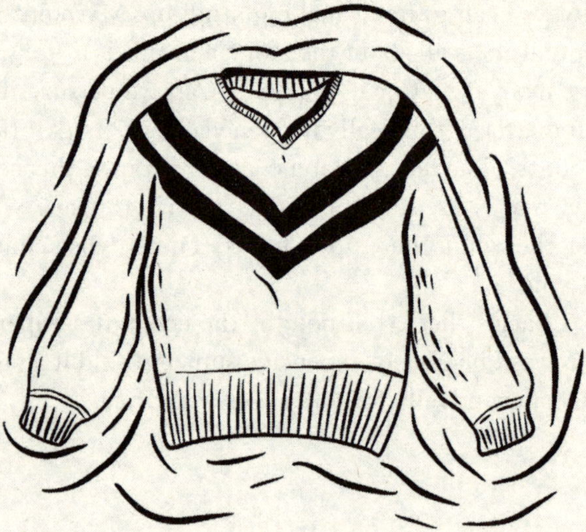

The Sweater

FEDERICA LOOKS JUST SO PERFECT. STRAIGHT BLONDISH HAIR, a cute button of a nose, pink lips that seem always ready for a kiss and bright, light blue eyes that stare at you from some distant place. Two sapphires, really. If you look deep enough into them, you might see an arctic glacier melting into the sunset. She's dressed in the most expensive Italian designers. Valentino, Prada, Giorgio Armani. I mean, everyone knows her father's company is producing their clothes. His factory is where they cut, stitch and manufacture the beautiful garments that are making a mark in the world of fashion right now. It's so clear that this decade is totally owned by Italian style. Everyone I know is convinced that the eighties will be remembered as the decade of Italian style. And yes, New Wave and, I know, the shoulder pads. I know those won't last. Too bulky, really. They make everyone look like football players. But Federica and I must wear them. It's the thing now. And we are wearing them even here, in the mountains.

I've been here for ten days now, in this quaint and breathtaking mountain house, built by Federica's father in the Ayas Valley, with killer views of the Matterhorn and the

Monte Rosa. Mountain vacations are like a bubble in time, everything is different, and anything can happen.

We've come here to the Alps to ski, but there's still a lot of fun to be had. The local boys seem a bit rough around the edges, but they're pretty hot anyway. Strong, muscular, all that hiking up and down in the summer and skiing all day in winter does marvels for their back muscles and thighs.

We went out with two brothers the other night, the Chasseurs. They have these weird French names here. I ended up with the less chatty of the two, of course. Federica got the short-cropped blond-haired Alpine guide. She told me later she drank so much grappa and Génépi liqueur that she woke up under a cold shower with him. She must've passed out. I didn't really feel like going all the way with the other brother. I mean, I would've, but only because I don't want Federica to think that I judge her for having slept with the older one.

The morning after, we were sitting at breakfast with her family. 'Stefano, can you hand me that croissant, please,' I asked Federica's brother. This autumn he dodged the mandatory military draft by corrupting an Army general with his father's money. And got caught. The trial is set for next summer. Federica already told me they found a judge they can bribe. This glitch in his life is not really holding Stefano back. He's always wired up. He's snorted so much cocaine by now that he always seems to be on it.

'Hey, Giorgia,' he said while tossing me a croissant across the table, 'did I tell you about that time I stole a yellow lifesaver from an airplane flying back from New York?'

'Yes, you did. And you got caught. And you pulled strings, the lifesaver's, and others, I know, very funny, ha ha, yes.'

Stefano laughed, but no one else did. Not even his mother who always defends him against the entire world.

Federica's older sister was the most serious one at the table. Even her name sounds more serious, Roberta. A bit masculine sounding. She's frowning all the time. She thinks it makes her look more like Brooke Shields. She has the same skilfully bleached blonde hair, even finer features, paler skin. She looks even more Swedish than the rest of this Northern Italian family.

They are all obsessed with this blondness. And yet all they can think about is getting a tan, relaxing in the sun while holding aluminium foil sheets, so they can tan under their chin.

'Isn't it weird that we are all trying to become darker, and yet there's no one with naturally dark skin here?' I asked at the table. Roberta broke out laughing.

'Did I tell you the story of Black Cicciobello?' she asked me. Seeing my puzzled expression, she started to tell it.

I mean, I know what Black Cicciobello is; everyone does. It is a kind of doll that was popular at the beginning of the eighties, like four years ago, basically. I don't know who had the idea of making a black doll in Italy. Some idealist hippies from the seventies, probably. Whatever the reason, Roberta and Federica's uncle, who lived in Milan and not in the forgotten little industrial town stuck at the foot of the hills where we will all have to go back to after Christmas, came home to find that his daughter had convinced the nanny to buy her a Black Cicciobello. It was a cute little doll, with big, innocent eyes, pouty lips, and a nice shade of dark brown.

'In the morning,' Roberta said, 'Carlottina woke up, but she couldn't find her Cicciobello. She was crying, poor thing.

Uncle told her that Cicciobello had gone back to his mother, in Africa. "It is only right, after all, isn't it, Carlottina?" he asked her. She eventually got over it ... But do you want to know what actually happened to Black Cicciobello?' Roberta asked.

'What happened?' I asked.

'At night Uncle had dug a deep hole in the garden, and buried Cicciobello.' They all laughed.

What is it with us Northern Italians and our admiration for blond people? I think it's because so many of us think we can pass. Don't we get it that it's all because, after the Romans got decimated by malaria, we were conquered for centuries by Normans, Germans, Gauls, Franks and similar blond barbarians, who put their kids in the castles of our peninsula to rule ruthlessly over us and tax us, the darker kind, filled with Arab, Asian, and African blood and DNA we never want to acknowledge?

Cicciobello's story made me look at my forearms, which always seem too dark and too hairy. I then caught myself noticing in the mirror my wavy black hair which never seems to find a proper hairdo, and my nose ...well, my nose ... I would be a prime candidate for a nose job, as I know it is the most distinctive feature on my face. Some of the harsher boys sometimes say things like, 'how do you know Giorgia will be here in five minutes? Because I just saw the tip of her nose turning the corner'. They laugh. Is it actually funny? I think I would probably find it funny if they were not talking about my nose. But they are.

I am the exact opposite of Federica, Roberta, Stefano and this entire fair-skinned, light-haired (although bleached) family of thin-nosed patricians. I mean, they are, like, totally proletarian, actually. The father was a simple textile worker in the big factory in our town. One of many farmers-turned-workers. But he was sly and fast and rode up the chain of command quickly. And then, in the late seventies, he opened his own sweatshop. He was one of those slaves who decided the way out of slavery was to become a slave owner himself. Reverse Spartacus, they call him.

Roberta had become one of the most sought-after single girls in our town. She's now dating Raffaele. He is old money. I mean, what's left of what appears as old money. He walks with his chin up in the air, like he's trying to reach the tip of the bell tower during the six o'clock strolls where we all show off our designer clothes, the Timberland shoes, the Loden coats, the Moncler down jackets and such. But really, Raffaele's old money comes from a grandfather who was nothing more than a tailor. Not all that noble, after all. But Raffaele thinks he's the Count of Hot Shitland.

When Roberta and Raffaele walk arm in arm on Main Street, everyone turns around to envy them. Who knows what great exclusive parties they go to? Who knows on what exotic, wonderful vacation they are invited? Cortina, Cote d'Azur, New York, helicopter skiing in Canada. That's the latest I heard.

The thing is (might as well tell you), Raffaele is my cousin. It's so strange because as he sits across the table, he totally avoids eye contact with me. It's as if he was embarrassed to have such a funky-haired, dark and loud cousin. I'm a reminder that the whole aristocratic bullshit story he lives by is a bunch of bona fide baloney.

It makes me want to be blond like Roberta and Federica. I want my Blue Lagoon too, with a sexy, curly blond boy, truth be told. But it's impossible; bleached blond hair would look way too much on me. So here, at this table, I'm sort of the poorest of the lot, invited to take part in a lifestyle I can't afford. And I absolutely adore it. I love it. I can't believe Federica picked me, of all our friends, to spend Christmas vacation in the Alps. Maybe it's because we share our deepest secrets with each other.

She told me everything about her youngest sister, Silvia, always sitting quietly at the end of the table. She's, like, seven years younger than us. Leaner, taller and flatter chested than her sisters and mother. Truly regal, but with zero snootiness. A kid still, but supercool. Everyone likes her. She keeps safely out of the family squabbles, in her saner world.

So, Federica told me it's pretty likely she's not their daddy's daughter. Federica's mom likes men. It's not really a secret. Sometimes, she brings her lover and his wife on their family sailboat vacations in the Adriatic Sea when they sail down to Yugoslavia. Federica's father must know what's going on. Maybe they're an open couple. I dunno. I know that I've seen them sleep in separate beds here in the mountains and back in our town too. Which, to me, is kind of weird. I would hate it if my parents slept in separate rooms. I can't picture my mother accepting that. She's all over my father. Adores him. Or seems to. But what does anyone know, really, about what goes on in a marriage? Well, I know what's *not* going on between Federica's parents. Sex. Not my business. But still pretty dark if you ask me. Not something really romantic to look forward to in life. Like a successful advertisement for what to avoid, with Federica's mom constantly and violently berating her husband in front of Raffaele and me. We're not part of this family. So, keep us out of this.

I can see Federica suffers from seeing them fight like this. Not just because it's embarrassing as hell, irritating and ultimately dull, but also because she remembers, or wants to think she remembers, a time when things worked. Federica has the energy of her mother and father put together. She's the first one leading the hiking group, when we go for a long trek in the summer in these most inspiring mountains, so different from the Dolomites I'm more used to. The Dolomites are all vertical drama, as they quickly take you up in the clouds in a world apart, walls and walls of rock that become pink, orange, purple at dawn and at sunset, and then get dark grey in the storm or shine bright in the moonlight. On the Alps, it's like riding on the back of gigantic mammoths. They are pyramids that begin in the plains of Piedmont and build up all the way to Switzerland and France. It's full of light, here in Val d'Ayas, everything exposed to the scrutiny of the sky.

When I see Federica leading the treks that etch their way up into the forest, she makes me think of a joyful elf taking me to her enchanted kingdom where everything will be better than this. Our future.

Do I love her? As a friend. I don't think of her as anything more. I'm not attracted to her sexually. At least, I don't think so. I like to hug her. I like to touch her light, straight hair. I like how her perfume mixes with her clothes and skin. I love how she dresses. I find the gold bracelets with silver screws that both she and Roberta wear – a shackled shaped gift from their mother – just so amazing. She has the best skirts, pants, shirts, sweaters. It's not just that I wish I had the money her family has. I wish I had her taste to choose those clothes. What would they look like on me?

Tonight, Raffaele, who is already nineteen, will be driving us to a restaurant at the pass leading to the next valley. In the summer, local boys like the Chaussers slide down this road in sturdy little skateboards. They are actually small sleighs with wheels. They lie face-up on them and whizz down the mountains, breaking with the heels of their sneakers. One of the Chasseurs brother's best friends was killed by a car coming up the road last summer.

Raffaele and Roberta sit at one corner of the table, whispering to each other. Stefano keeps going to the bathroom and comes back talking nonsense. Federica and I make fun of people at other tables, one of our favourite pastimes. I am happy. I wish life could always be just like this.

The day after, at breakfast, a fight breaks out. This time it's Federica and Roberta.

'You always take my sweater without asking!' Federica yells.

'I don't like your stupid little fake hippie sweaters, are you mad?' Roberta yells back.

'You borrowed it two months ago and I had to come get it from you. Now it's gone again. Where is it?'

'I told you I didn't take it!'

'Fucking bitch!' Federica reaches over the table and grabs a handful of Roberta's beautiful blond hair and pulls. A part of me rejoices. Federica is so cool and gutsy. Roberta scratches Federica in the neck. Raffaele tries to break them apart, shrieking. Stefano is laughing his head off. Young Silvia looks at them and sighs. The father keeps banging his flat palm on the table and yells, unheard, 'Stop it! Stop it! Stop it now!' The mother yells a very loud shriek, 'Inbeeeciiiils!' Eventually Federica and Roberta are separated. Roberta storms out of the room, followed by Raffaele who whines a pathetic 'my little baby, wait!' They disappear. I don't think I'm the only one who knows that, in the middle of the night, Roberta leaves her room and goes down the two flights of steps and into Raffaele's guest room in the basement. He's staying right next to my room. I hear their bed squealing like a tiny mouse in a trap.

It's the last day of the holidays. Tomorrow we'll drive all the way across Northern Italy, back to our town.

At night, Federica and I talk until three in the morning, excited about the new school term and about the new alliances we want to forge with friends in school. We are already planning a party for next weekend.

After breakfast, as we load up the cars, I let my bag drop to the floor of the driveway, having failed to properly latch my stuff. I have an old, battered leather bag with a metallic latch, a model they stopped making in the sixties. It was given to me as part of the belongings of my great aunt, who died last year, one of those leather objects from the pre-plastic era. I thought it looked cool, although I can tell Raffaele thinks I look like one of those poor Italians who had to leave for America to look for work. The luggage slips from my hand and hits the icy ground. Everything pops out. Roberta is the first one who notices that Federica's missing sweater is hidden among my things. I'm immediately dragged back into the house and made to sit on the sofa, as Roberta begins to interrogate me in front of an embarrassed Federica. I know my friend forgives me. I know Federica understands I took her sweater because I love her, as a friend. Maybe she understands that the thing I would like most in the world is to be her. Yes, with the superficial, neurotic, snobbish sister yelling at me, the silly brother who talks too much nonsense and the half-sister everyone knows is from an out-of-wedlock relationship, and that spiteful mother and wimpy father. I don't care. I just wish I were Federica. Not like her. Her. That's why … that sweater…

The most shocked of them all, the one who doesn't say a word but stands as if frozen in a corner is Raffaele. He has implanted himself in this wealthy family with his air of being above it all, and the fact that I, his cousin, turned out to be a kleptomaniac freak, will now raise suspicions about his intentions towards his family and Roberta. He and Roberta are doomed.

This is why Roberta is so incredibly angry at me, not because of the clump of hair Federica pulled from her skull the day before, unjustly accusing her of having stolen her sweater.

That's why Raffaele now looks out the window with a sad face, staring at the amazing pink light emerging from the early morning sunrise that covers the slopes of the Matterhorn like a Japanese cartoon.

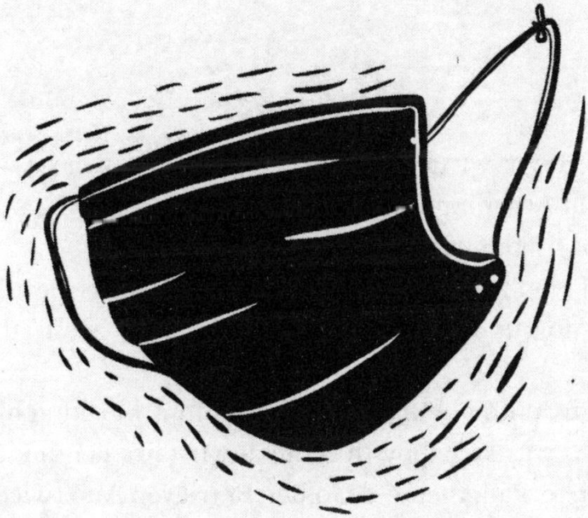

The Mask

'YOU MUST WEAR YOUR MASK!' SAID THE ANGRY MAN. HE was standing exactly one metre from Franco, as mandated by the latest government decree.

'But I don't have one,' Franco answered as he tried to keep the dog under control. 'Stay put, Rocco, wait!' the boy said.

The guy didn't budge and stared at him, blocking his way.

Franco was so happy that the downstairs neighbour had asked him to walk their old Golden Retriever. And twice a day. Because of the lockdown, the boy who had stolen Franco's dog-walking job was now confined to his apartment across town. That meant five euros a walk, or ten euros a day for Franco – a sum that came in handy since his parents had stopped giving him an allowance now that he had turned sixteen. He had to find ways to fund his weekends. Although no one had weekends anymore.

Since the average age of people dying had begun to decrease, he had become more and more nervous about walking Rocco. When he did go out, he stayed away from people as much as possible. During the first days of the epidemic, before it was upgraded to a pandemic, he had seen only homeless people on the streets. One of them looked like a caveman – he had rolled a chicken bone into his oily fringe. Another bum yelled at Franco, out of the blue, from 100 metres across Piazza Santa Maria in Trastevere:

'Ciaooo! How are youuu?! All good?!'

Franco screamed back: 'I'm fine, thank you! How are you?'

Then a doctor from the shelter had tested positive and Franco started to keep even further away from the homeless. He used to dread going out, preferring to stay in his blue-painted room playing video games, just like all his friends. But during the first week he began to get restless and now, he could hardly wait to take Rocco out. But … he was conflicted between needing some air and the fear of virus-carrying droplets sprayed by asymptomatic carriers, the worst enemies.

The guy with the mask didn't look like a bum. He was one of those fifty-something men who had slowly begun to come out in the open more often, with the excuse of buying cigarettes or medicines.

'You must put your mask on!' he insisted.

'Look, I don't even have a mask.'

'You must wear a mask!'

'I'm sorry, I don't have one. Masks now cost thirty-six euros. I don't have thirty-six euros to spend on a mask you must change every eight hours, okay? But even if I did, there are no masks in the shops right now, don't you know?'

'You have to wear a mask!' the man screamed.

Tightening his grip on Rocco's leash, Franco looked the man straight in the eyes and began to cough steadily towards him. Slowly, continuously. The man jumped back, nervously, yelling 'Hey, watch it!' before dashing away.

The encounter had made Franco irritated and tense. There was no law forcing people to wear masks. Besides, only the infected were supposed to wear them. There was so much confusing information swirling around. Some said wearing masks was worse; some swore only sick people should wear them; others, like that guy, thought everyone should always wear one.

Life had changed overnight. No, that's not true. Life had changed slowly. At first, no one believed it would reach Rome. People were forwarding WhatsApp jokes: 'Can't get a table at a crowded restaurant? We can rent you a coughing Chinese so everybody will leave!' said a Neapolitan voice in a recorded message, coughing.

When the virus started killing eight people a day in Lombardy, Europeans and Southern Italians used the same joke with people from Milan. When more than 300 people started dying every day, in all of Italy, no one, except the French, kept joking about it. They had made a video of an old Italian man sliding a pizza out of a brick oven and coughing a green pesto-like glob of mucus on it. The French ambassador had to be photographed eating pizza with the Italian foreign minister to calm the situation. Nevertheless, they kept a metre apart from each other. The Austrians blocked the borders to keep their ventilators in and infected Italians out. Someone in England said self-isolation was just a sorry excuse for those lazy Italians to stay home from work. Europe was crumbling.

When the French started dying, the jokes stopped altogether.

Franco was still looking for masks for himself and his mother, but they were sold out within two days, across the entire country. The black market was filled with fakes or with masks otherwise used only for DIY and gardening – not for medical use. The Carabinieri arrested dozens of people peddling them at exorbitant prices. His mother had written to Franco's father, who was stuck in quarantine in Qatar where he had been on a business trip. None to be found there, either. Finally, Franco's aunt in Los Angeles, Elena, was able to send some, as the pandemic had yet to fully reach them.

The one positive thing out of all this, Franco thought, was that even though in the first week of lockdown his friends, his mother and the neighbours had started to become more nervous, like the man in the mask in Piazza San Callisto, by the third week people started to sing songs at the same time of day. Balcony and courtyard concerts commenced at six in the evening and at eight and ten at night throughout the nation. Before, he'd rarely meet the neighbours in the building across from his. He had caught a glimpse of them regularly and for years, of course. They were the familiar faces you sometimes say hello to, when your gazes lock and you're too close to avoid them, but whose names you'd never know. Or care to know.

Now they were all singing the same songs at the same time every day. The balcony songs, they were called.

One evening, as he quietly sang and watched everyone else sing together, it seemed to him as if they were celebrating their victory over a virus, rather than being afraid of catching it. What kind of virus had kept them away from all this, away from such communal joy, found simply by opening their windows and singing with those who had been strangers before? He knew they must have had a virus: the virus of ambition, of busyness, of the constant need for entertainment and the desire for useless things. Perhaps it was just that … They somehow looked healed, as if they finally had let go of something they did not need, something, or many things, that had been weighing them down.

A friend on Insta asked: 'How many of you are having nightmares every night? I keep dreaming of things falling out of my hands, of losing control of everything.'

Maybe people were secretly relieved and glad to have the chance to lose control, a feeling balanced by tension, by the fear of death.

Luca, a friend of his parents, posted: 'We both have nightmares, every night, Sara and I, but when we wake up, we realize reality is worse.'

But was it? Yes, it was, yet something strange was happening to people, something good, despite the bad.

Franco felt stronger than the nightmares. He did pull-ups and push-ups every morning and every afternoon. Online classes, which at first felt like a joke, became something to look forward to, a moment of connection. All those faces together on the screen … And, on the plus side, there was so much more time to play video games online with friends.

His father played the stock market, and had told Franco, on a recent Skype chat from Doha, that he must think proactively, stay strong and positive. His father was like that: constantly, untiringly, boringly encouraging. Franco was fed up with all this encouragement, all the time.

'You need even more strength than normal,' his father insisted. 'Think of how the world will change. Who will go down? But, also, who will benefit? There's always someone benefitting. Which stocks would you bet on right now, for example? What is your intuition on this? You've always been good at it.'

Well, easy, he said, dump airlines and tourism. Buy cannabis and alcohol stocks. Companies making condoms and diapers. People will be having a lot more sex, that's for sure. Not that Franco had any experience. Not yet at least. He didn't like to talk about that. He was waiting for the right person, although now…

But it made sense. People will want to celebrate and screw their way out of this. Like those singers on the balcony. Buy pharmaceuticals. Not just for vaccines. Once everyone is immunized, that's money down the drain. Nor for tests, it won't play long unless you're shorting. But tranquillizers. The world was undergoing massive trauma and would need to be sedated.

As usual, when he was talking to someone on Skype, instead of looking at the person's face, in this case his father's, he was studying his own. He realized he was, again, obsessively adjusting his unruly head of hair. It was always too puffy. But he couldn't cut it shorter because it would expose his forehead, which was impressive. Franco also realized, studying himself on the screen while his father talked from a time zone where it was already dusk, that he still looked too much like Harry Potter. It had never been cute. He'd always hated that sanctimonious Harry Potter who everyone else seemed to love. New frames hadn't helped. When his father had taken him on a trip to Japan, some people on the streets had pointed at him saying 'Haru Potteru!'

When would they be able to take another trip like that? Would the world ever go back to that kind of normal?

Franco had been surprised there hadn't been more violence and anarchy, like in the dystopian movies they had watched gleefully over the past few years. How long would the balcony songs last? Two, three weeks, a month perhaps. Then? Would it turn ugly? What about spring when the sun comes out? How would they keep people home, inside?

And what about all the frail people, and those who were already slightly neurotic, like his mother, who was showing signs of more instability. Or his cousin, for example, who was convinced he had the virus. He had been to the ER so often that when he walked in, they would say, 'Hey, there's Sandro again!'

This happened before they closed the ER to walk-ins like him. Sandro then started to check his temperature every two hours. But no fever. Yet he felt he had this weird pain in his chest. Franco explained via WhatsApp that these were not the right symptoms. Sounded more like panic attacks.

Then Franco lost his patience: 'We're all being asked to just take a fucking break, Sandro, how hard could that be. Just re-evaluate and rest. That's all!'

As he said this, he wondered how true it was. *Was* that all? Of course not.

One afternoon, when they went out to shop for food with the printed pass, Franco's mother asked him if they could take a short walk by the river. She always walked briskly, as if chased by some invisible ghost. In public, she often kept a fixed grin, but you couldn't see it now, as they were both wearing the black masks sent by Franco's aunt. He had started to wear his all the time, his face disappearing under the cloud of hair, the big eyeglasses and the dark band across his chin. Sometimes, when he was alone in his room, he got so anxious that he put it on, even though there was no need, just to feel reassured and to settle his breathing.

As they were walking along the Tiber, the waters below sounded crisper than usual, the fresh March air felt even fresher, and, as he lowered the mask for an instant to breathe freely, the trees seemed to rejoice in the wind. The disappearance of the persistent flow of traffic that had flanked Rome's ancient river made it all so quiet now.

His mother suddenly yanked his elbow and begged him to cross the street.

'Quick, quick, quick!'

'What's wrong?'

'I've never told you this, but I'm terrified of … those…' She pointed to a row of trees lining up on the side of the Lungotevere.

'Pine trees?'

'Yes. Sorry. I've had this fear since I was a child but…'

They shuffled over to the other sidewalk, turned right at Piazza Trilussa, eerily devoid of its crowd of pot-smokers, drunkards and musicians who cheered up the evenings. No more trattoria, their outdoor tables busy with customers sitting in front of deep dishes filled with linguine. Even the busy Piazza della Malva was empty and, most painful of all, now even the La Boccaccia white pizza-to-go counter had shut. This was one of the things that hurt the most, not having his daily focaccia-like delicacy on the way back from Virgilio High, just over the bridge.

The person who seemed least disturbed by all this was the one at higher risk – his seventy-eight-year-old grandmother, who lived in a city up north, smack in the heart of the Red Zone. They Skyped every day after lunch when she would be drinking her coffee on her sunlit balcony, laughing, in good spirits. She said she'd been used to self-isolation since her husband died twenty-five years ago. *Nonna* practised yoga, watched her TV soaps, reread some classics, and went for short walks with her neighbour (keeping a metre between themselves) and her little Boston Terrier. 'So far, so good,' she would say.

But then hospitals started filling up, reaching overcapacity. 'Patient number one' – a thirty-eight-year-old semi-pro runner – was hospitalized undiagnosed for the virus and hospitals in Lombardy were the first to register dozens of deaths among staff as well as patients. Doctors and nurses had to be tubed up to ventilators and took precedence over the elderly. It was just protocol. Unless, of course, the elderly were doctors or nurses. And even medical staff who had tested positive were called back to work if they had less than 38 C fever. They had to turn 10,000 young medical students into practising doctors, overnight. Then people in their sixties and fifties started to lose the privilege of using life-saving machines. As the numbers went up, the new death tally was announced every evening at six – the exact time the chorus of national anthems could be heard from balconies.

During the first week, Franco kept playing football with his friends. Everyone was on edge, and a good game helped shave away the tension. It was thought the virus was killing only older people. At least, that's what younger people wanted to believe. Then someone said it won't kill in hot weather. Then tropical countries proved to be vulnerable also, and then teenagers began to be hospitalized. Pneumonia and … gone. No more football games.

This was when Franco started to feel a little discomfort in his throat. First, he thought it was his ear. Just an infection returning from three months ago, when the doctor had prescribed antibiotic drops. He was not going to go paranoid like his cousin Sandro. He felt a nasty discomfort as he swallowed. The day after, a slight feeling of asphyxia. His forehead was hot. The new decree made it mandatory to report these symptoms to the emergency number. After two days with 37.5 C fever, his mother dialled the number. She had chewed her lip over it but decided to go ahead after a sleepless night. This was a dangerous move. Franco knew of kids his age who had called the number, had gone in for a test and never came out. You couldn't even have their ashes back. How could he tell if his shortness of breath was the virus or if it was just … panic?

Silently he started to cry in his room, with the door locked. He just wanted to be with his friends. This is what he missed the most. To be able to hang out, like a few weeks before. That's all. If only everyone could sing together every day, but also still be able to see each other for a stroll or at Bar Settimiano, where everyone had known him since he was a child…

He was asked to go to a testing centre. Immediately. And told not to take anything special, to just show up, alone. It was nearby, in the hospital in Piazza San Cosimato where he played football with his friends, before Rome and every other city had turned into deserts and before every balcony sported a tri-coloured Italian flag in the largest show of patriotism since Fascism 100 years before, and before the waters in the Venice canal looked pristine, as the world's media reported, trying to find something positive to divulge. Everyone talked of Italian excellence in handling the pandemic, yet Franco thought: *If we're so excellent, how come we have more dead people than all the other countries?*

Franco pressed the buzzer of the small gate. A lady in full protective gear came out, opened it, and led him to a large room filled with rows of empty beds, where a few other patients were waiting. They were all keeping themselves at least one metre apart. When the nurse came back, she called out his name and took him to an examination room where they stuck a cotton swab up his nose.

'It might feel like your eyes want to pop out,' the nurse said, through her mask and goggles. 'But be patient, it'll only take five seconds, even though it'll feel like an hour of torture.'

He squirmed.

'Be still, please ... There, done...'

Another nurse walked him back to the room, taking him through an enchanted cloister filled with olive and fir trees. This little Eden led to a wing of the building called *Malattie Infettive*. Once back in the large room, the nurse gave him two pills to swallow, and a paper cup filled with water.

'We should know the results in about twenty-four hours, if not sooner,' she said.

'Okay. So, I have to come back tomorrow?'

'No, no. You have to stay here with the others until we have the results.'

'But ... I don't have anything to sleep in. No toothbrush, nothing...'

'Someone can bring it in. You have a phone, right?'

An hour later, his mother arrived with his package – but she had to stay outside. She was not allowed to see him, not even through a window. Franco lay in a bed trying not to think, or to cry again – he didn't want to embarrass himself.

He felt someone standing close to his bed.

'I told you,' a voice, coming from about a metre away. 'You should've worn a mask.'

He looked up. The eyes looked familiar. But he couldn't tell who this person was. Perhaps a friend of his father, he thought, spreading a smile which died on his face as soon as he realized who it was. The angry guy, of course. He was also a patient there, waiting for results.

'It doesn't seem to have helped you much,' Franco said, through his own black mask.

'I only hope I haven't caught it from you. If I did…'

'I guess we'll find out tomorrow.'

Then the main lights went off. Franco checked his phone. It was already ten at night.

How could anyone sleep at a moment like this? He certainly couldn't, especially after that veiled threat. He could hear the others fidgeting, tossing and turning, all of them one metre – or more – apart.

At eleven, the lights came back on, suddenly. Everyone's eyes took a second to adjust as the main door opened and the female nurse walked in, followed by four muscled-up male nurses in protective gear.

'We have the results,' she said. 'All the negatives can leave; all the positives have to follow me. Negatives, you're asked to self-quarantine in your own rooms, if you have one at home, or, if you don't, to stay at least one metre away from everyone else for another two weeks. If you have symptoms again, come back here for a second test.'

Then she called their names and handed them a piece of paper. The man from Piazza San Callisto looked at the note, then immediately glanced at him. Franco clutched his paper but was afraid to look.

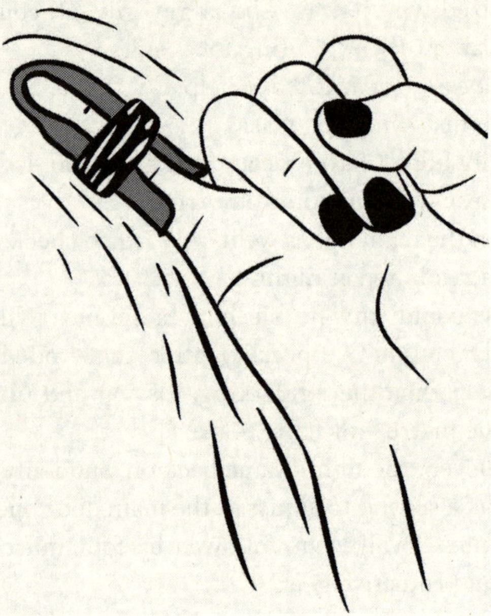

The Splint

TRISTAN IS A HIGH SCHOOL MUSIC TEACHER WHO IS NOT particularly fond of teenagers, nor of teaching. He used to be fond of music, he says. The strangers around him are listening attentively to his anecdote. A Spanish man sitting next to him at the dinner table enquires about the splint that keeps his pinkie finger raised, as if he were a coquettish lady sipping evening tea with co-conspirators on a dark winter day.

He has been invited to dinner by the girlfriend he met through *The Guardian*'s personals ads. Tristan is really trying to make it work and he has a surprise in store for his date this evening, but it is too early to reveal it. The story he must tell now will be the perfect preamble for it, though.

It all began with his brand new, expensive racing bicycle, Tristan says. He had saved for months from his teacher's salary to buy this beauty. He had crouched down on the moustache handlebar and started down the road with such bravado that people in his London neighbourhood thought he'd turned into a bike messenger, which he sort of looked like, with his trimmed beard, shabby-chic, sporty clothes, and hidden sneer – remnants of a musician's vanity.

He sprinted down the road, breathing in the cold air, which flew through his hipster beard and up his dilated nostrils, shoulders clenched in full control of that new mechanical jewel when *wham!* a London cabbie slammed right into his front wheel.

He tumbled, crashed, collapsed, embarrassed himself, and jumped up ready for a fight, but then suddenly he felt a strong, sharp pain burning in his hand. His pinkie was pulsating madly, like it had a heart of its own.

In the emergency room, they'd been very efficient in welcoming him, not making him wait too long, and providing clear information on protocol and procedure to be followed. He loved the National Health Service, he said. But when he was asked to state his name, the person in charge typed Tristan's name on the keyboard, stared at the screen, and then looked at him with a quizzical expression.

'Tristan Campbell?'

'Yes.'

'Tristan Campbell born in Yorkshire, January sixth, nineteen seventy-six?'

'Yes, that's right.'

'How are you feeling, sir?'

'What do you mean: how am I feeling? I'm in the emergency room. I was just run over by a cabby; I've just told you that. My left hand hurts. It hurts a lot, as I've said when I walked in. And you ask me how I'm feeling?'

'Yes, sir.'

'Well, I'm in fucking dire pain, love!' Tristan tried to add a smile but couldn't muster enough spirit to pull it off.

'I'm just asking because it says here that you are dead.'

'I'm dead?'

'Yes, sir.'

'It says there that I'm dead?'

'Yes, sir. It says here that Mr Tristan Campbell, born in Yorkshire on January sixth, nineteen seventy-six, actually died of complications in a Yorkshire hospital twenty years ago after surgery on his kidneys.'

Tristan stared at the nurse.

'I did have surgery on my kidneys in Yorkshire twenty years ago, but I have, evidently, survived it, haven't I?'

'Not according to our records, sir.'

At the dinner, Tristan proceeds to expand on his discovery of having been unknowingly dead for twenty years, delighting his newfound friends at the dinner table. His date is radiant and admires him for being able to hold the easily distracted attention of this privileged bunch for such a long time with the fantastic story of his own death.

It had taken him a long time to convince the British bureaucracy that he was actually alive, Tristan says to the dinner guests. He had to travel to Yorkshire, visit the hospital, ask to see the original record, and verify who had signed his death certificate. He still wasn't sure who had declared him dead and why. He said he thought he must've pissed off one of the nurses at the time.

'I wasn't exactly the likeable kind,' he admits to his listeners, putting on his most likeable face. Which is still a bit unlikeable.

Eventually, he was able to set the record straight and felt like he was born again, he says. But this entire process of discovering he had been dead for twenty years, the deep symbolism of it all, did not elude him. It reawakened a formerly sensitive Tristan, the young musician who played guitar in a band, who had moved to London to cut a record, which never got made. He realized he had given up on his dream of being a musician and had turned to teaching as an alternative to survive in London, exactly after that kidney operation.

'I really had been dead for twenty years,' he says, 'or, rather, my true dream had.'

He could not let this fortuitous discovery pass without doing something about it, he says. 'When they were putting this splint on my pinkie in that hospital, I felt this was my chance to be reborn,' he says to the adoring dozen, the Spanish fellow with his mouth half-open in awe of this cheap symbolism.

'I understood I must sing again and play music, just like I did before I allegedly died and moved to London and was forced to teach music to teenagers to make a living.'

Tristan says he just quit his job and picked up singing and playing and composing music again.

'Oh, play something for us, I beg you!' screams the hostess, excited her girlfriend has brought such an original raconteur to her dinner table.

'Well, my hand is a bit handicapped, as you can see, but I have composed this new song over the last few days, because of … well, you'll hear about it, if I'm able to get the chords right.'

Tristan caresses the strings of the classical guitar that has been lying in the corner of the dining room. He extracts a naive ballad from it, about dolphins who swim in the sea and an albatross who doesn't want to fly anymore but is lured by another beautiful dolphin to try once again. As the albatross soars in those oceanic skies, so does the singer, who decides it's time to sing again, and it's time to love again.

As he finishes his last lines, and as the last notes stop reverberating in the silent dining room, there is timid, sparse and embarrassed clapping.

Then everyone looks away quickly and desperately tries to find a new topic of conversation.

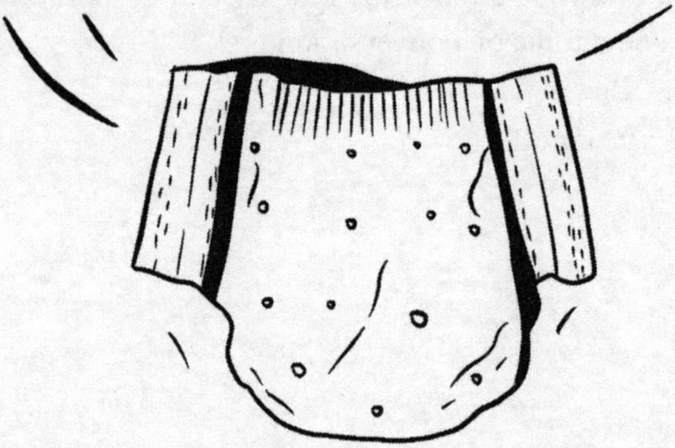

The Diaper

WHENEVER HE WAS ASKED WHY HE HAD BECOME A vegetarian, Gustav always told the same story. It was the Spring of 2004. He could recollect this with precision because what happened involved not only his partner Anne, a photographer he had met and fallen in love with in 2001, but also their child Hector who, when Gustav became a vegetarian, was only four months old.

Gustav and Anne had moved to the Quartier Latin in Paris for two months. They rented an apartment from a famous professor of philosophy, George Sansjambes, who taught at the nearby Sorbonne University and who had left the city for a sabbatical in Rome. It was a narrow, steep four-floor walk-up, leading to a two-floor duplex with high windows facing the postcard panorama of Parisian roofs. It wasn't an easy climb, with shopping bags and baby Hector in their arms, but Gustav and Anne were athletic and, although already in their late thirties, were both swimming twice a week, back in their hometown of Lyon.

Gustav had taken advantage of a three-month paternity leave from the telecommunication company where he had worked for the past two years as a marketing creative, while Anne had hoped to jump-start her career in photography, a concept that in the pre-Instagram era still seemed possible. She had set up meetings to show her portfolio to editors at newspapers, magazines and photo agencies, hoping to get hired.

As a teenager, Gustav had been on vacation in the Quartier Latin with his girlfriend from Arles, Nathalie. The narrow streets filled with students, bohemians and professors made him feel like he had entered the set of a Godard movie or Truffaut film, *Nouvelle Vague* directors whose work he'd worshipped when he was in his twenties. The smell of flowers in the market, the champagne bottles lined up in the quality shops, the brasseries on the corner … everything reeked of a nostalgic emotion he was addicted to. As he took in all these details, his chest puffed up with oxygen and he felt his arms fill with warmth, as if he had dipped them in a hot bath. His pores were opening to take in all this beauty.

Gustav and Anne had been so elated about their Parisian Spring, when they had driven into the city from Lyon, as the wide expanse of the metropolis opened up for them in the sunset, that they started to sing a cheesy Parisian song from the forties that many French know by heart: *'C'est la romance de Paris!'*

They had opted not to get married. As Gustav explained to anyone who asked, he had always been against the need to have society sanction personal feelings. And Anne had actually gotten married – and divorced a year later – when she was twenty-one. She confessed this to Gustav only when they were registering Hector's birth, and the clerk asked her if she'd been married before. She had been embarrassed about it. She had married a man ten years older than her.

In those days, she had slept around quite a bit and was convinced she must've gotten AIDS. Her plan was to get married before dying. Of course, she hadn't been tested, nor were there any indications of her having contracted the disease, but at the time, she admitted, she was probably smoking too many joints of cheap hashish, snorting a bit too much coke mixed with too many vodka tonics and was most likely arriving at paranoid conclusions about her health. It had been, she told Gustav, as if she had been living under a thick, transparent, glass bell. She could see the outside world, but slightly distorted. The sounds coming through were not always understandable. The impulsive marriage to the older photo editor was over very soon. She vowed not to get married again. What was the point, really?

Gustav was in love with her and, even more, he was in love with the smiling, calm, sweet boy he had seen slip out of Anne's womb at the hospital in Lyon, after an entire night of labour, first alleviated with an epidural injection and then, when Hector had still seemed unwilling to face the world, with a caesarean section. Anne had been so fatigued by the strain of trying to push Hector out and by the after-effects of the drugs that she slept for twelve hours straight. That's why little Hector spent his first night on his father's chest, as Gustav had a little cot set up in Anne's hospital room.

The day after, Gustav walked back to their apartment to get a change of clothes for Anne. Their apartment was less than two kilometres from the clinic and Gustav was so charged with energy that he decided to walk home instead of getting on the bus. It was only while crossing the square near their apartment building that he lowered his gaze from the sky, heart galloping with paternal joy, and realized he was still wearing a pair of embarrassing green plastic hospital shoe covers.

This was also when he realized something truly life-changing had happened to him, that thing that almost every father had tried to explain to him before giving up, admitting they couldn't put it into words. Now he understood.

He also thought, for the first time in his immature life, that one day he was going to die. He'd never thought about his own death before. Not when his beloved grandfather had died, nor when his two cool, determined, and modern-thinking grandmothers had died. He had not thought about it even when he was six years old, and his best friend Antoine had died during surgery. Antoine was supposed to have one of his recalcitrant testicles dislodged from his groin and lowered into his tiny scrotum. It turned out the boy was one in a hundred thousand people who were deathly allergic to a specific type of anaesthesia used in the seventies in France. Antoine never woke up. Gustav had cried for hours when he'd been told, but it was out of despair for his friend, not out of fear for himself. All that was left in his memory of his best friend, now, was a photograph of a boy dressed in a small, black cowboy hat, a checked shirt, and a waistcoat, drawing something on a desk while smiling with two missing front teeth.

Becoming a father felt like truly growing up. Gustav saw his future with suddenly narrowed paths, options disappearing, possibilities vanishing as the responsibilities of this new life started to quickly crush him. And yet, as proven by his exhilarated gait through the centre of Lyon, he was not feeling heavy at all. Perhaps this rationalization of future possibilities was a good thing. The chemicals he felt springing within him, the mix of adrenaline and endorphins, and whatever else his glands must be squeezing into his blood in that moment, were simply bringing him to a level of excited ecstasy for life. Everything glowed. Especially Hector.

This is the feeling he was experiencing in that apartment in Rue Lavelle in the Quartier Latin, while he was changing Hector's diaper. He was also laughing silently, thinking about the collection of vintage porno magazines Anne had dug out from the philosophy professor's closet. The luminary had written a treatise on the pornography, so Gustav was trying to justify this discovery as field research of a serious academic, while Anne, who had ample first-hand knowledge of the lust of men, understood what it meant – an overgrown libido in constant need of fuel.

Gustav's attention was brought back to Hector, who kicked his little feet in the air while giggling. He unstrapped the diaper from his son's hips which revealed tiny droppings that Hector had produced. The baby was still in the phase where faeces do not take on that foul smell that only gets worse with age. No, it wasn't the sight of the poo that day, which made Gustav a vegetarian for the following ten years. It was something that happened after he wiped Hector clean, a manoeuvre which by now he had learned to do with only one hand.

It was while he handled Hector's tiny naked torso that an uncomfortable and shocking feeling began to creep into him, as an image formed in his mind, something he would not be able to erase for the next ten years.

It happened mid-afternoon, right after lunch. Anne had returned from her meeting carrying a fragrant roast chicken, a plump *poulet* she had fetched at the rotisserie down at the corner. She had to walk all the way around the block because between the rotisserie and the house there was a street lined with pines, and she had a peculiar phobia of those trees. There was even a fancy name for it: *dendrophobia.*

They had both eaten the little bird with the appetite of a couple who still made love often. Gustav had sunk the tip of his fingers through the ribs of the chicken, scraping the chest of all shreds of meat, stuffing his mouth, sucking the grease off his fingers. While chewing, Gustav had bitten the side of his tongue and tasted his blood mixed with the white meat.

Now, as he was holding Hector's tiny torso, after putting a clean diaper on him and massaging the baby with some talcum powder, he felt a shiver of horror traverse him. Hector and the chicken were the same thing. Sentient beings with feelings, with the same experience of life. Gustav realized that the chicken he had just eaten in such a famished rush had been a small chick, conceived by parents and, even more importantly, that that animal, having a rib cage that so resembled that of his son, was actually a being in no way different from a human. That chicken had lived. He had felt. He had rejoiced in the simple basic and common fact of being alive, taking pleasure from nourishment, from the warmth of a mother or perhaps even a father, from the joy of waking up, opening his eyes, and experiencing life through all senses.

That's when Gustav felt that all beings – chickens, pigs, cows, goats, sheep – all beings that we humans kill, skin, drain of blood, chop, quarter and prepare in a neat package for a counter, all of them had the experience of life. The same as us. He felt like a cannibal.

The day after, when Gustav and Anne took Hector out to get some fresh Parisian air in his stroller and stopped at the corner brasserie for lunch, Gustav found himself in front of a tourist menu with images of meat and fish glazed over by a special lighting effect, which Anne explained involved a cube of panels refracting light so as to make a dead fish look like one of the blond ladies in the professor's vintage porno magazines. It wasn't exactly nausea Gustav felt from what, until the day before, had been his favourite dish, the yummy *steak frites*; it was something deeper. It was a specific feeling, the feeling that his own flesh could be there, on that plate, garnished with crunchy, oily potato strips. He ordered a niçoise salad without tuna.

Two weeks later, Gustav and Anne found themselves with Hector in the Moroccan coastal town of Essaouira. They had gotten on an inexpensive flight from Paris to Marrakesh and rented a car at the airport. It was time to take a break from Paris, and Anne would also photograph the annual Berber music festival, which gathered musicians from all over the world. Gustav recognized the thick walls of the city where Orson Welles had shot *Othello*. He was aware of how much his own experience of architecture, cities and geography had been influenced by his exposure to literature and cinema. He felt he was culturally programmed and could not experience anything without a reference to an illustrated volume he read as a child, or a memorable movie he saw as a teenager, or a profound novel he read in his twenties.

They strolled down the huge wall circling the city, all the way to the harbour, among the fishermen's shacks, where you could sit on a simple wooden bench and dig into the catch of the day, freshly cooked in front of your nose. Distracted by the coastal African beauty of Essaouira, Gustav made the same mistake. He dug his fingers into the freshly fried fish and, as he began inching his digits into the fish bones, he felt the same discomfort as he had in Paris when he thought of the chicken. He could not finish what was on his plate. That ended his taste for fish too. For the next ten years, he couldn't eat anything that had eyes, so he stuck to a diet based on plants and their by-products.

Bizarrely, Hector grew up as one of the most carnivorous boys Gustav had ever met. Hector demanded ham or sliced sausages for breakfast, loved filet mignon, steaks, T-bone, chops, tortellini with meat, pasta with ragout. He made himself grilled salami and sandwiched it between two slabs of cheese instead of bread. He was a cholesterol vampire who loved trying the most exotic meats, crunchy little birds to be swallowed whole, fancy wild boar, tongue, intestines, tripe. The smellier and fouler, the better. It was as if Hector had become savagely carnivorous as a silent protest against what he saw as his father's weakness in dietary choices.

Gustav would cook these morsels of dead beings for his son, trying to turn his nose away because the sheer smell of these dead animals made him think of human flesh. But he did not want to impose on his son a strictly personal choice. He had become overly sensitive, and Anne started to feel more and more distanced from this new man who never went back to work in marketing, as he could not contribute to the promotion and sale of dead beings.

When Gustav and Anne separated, three awfully long years later, Anne made it a point to make sure that their son would not be tempted by what she considered a weak vegetarian diet, so she kept the refrigerator stuffed with the butcher's best cuts, with fresh fish and all the little corpses that so horrified her 'son's father', which was how she now referred to him when talking to her friends. In her eyes, Gustav's vegetarianism was proof of the weakness and fragility of the man she had decided to have a child with. She wanted to protect Hector from such misinformed insanity.

It wasn't until Anne realized she was hard of hearing that she understood why she had always felt like she lived under a glass bell. Nothing more complicated than a hearing problem. She started using hearing aids, married the philosophy professor from the Sorbonne and moved to the flat in Rue Lavelle. Hector grew up to be a rather happy boy in the Quartier Latin. When he turned 18, he decided to stop talking to his vegetarian father.

Meanwhile Gustav, on a vacation in Thailand a few years later, got sick to the stomach and had a craving for a burger. He ate two in a row and stopped being a vegetarian. Whenever he ate meat, he still felt the horror of chewing something that had been alive, a feeling, again, of cannibalism, but he decided to live with this ambiguity.

He dislocated the joint of his toe due to the side effects of gout.

DRIVER LICENSE
ID:
NAME
F

The Driver’s Licence

‘HEY, T. I’M ON THE PULL TONGHT. HERE’S PX OF MY DATE, in case somethng happens to me.thnkn of takng hm home. txt u later! wsh me luck! 😊’

Sohini liked the sound of it. ‘On the pull.’ There was something raunchy and erotic about it. And empowering. Ever since her mother died, she’d felt an even stronger need to be in charge. Maybe it was all the battles with her stepbrothers and stepsisters, competing for their billionaire dad’s attention. Now that her mother was gone, lost to a car accident while on vacation in Marbella, there was no one to whisper in her father’s ear about treating children equally. She was not the prettiest of the lot. Too short, too petite, too fierce, too angry, a quick mind ready to dish out sharp remarks. She also kept a perfectly toned body with a gym schedule she followed with Prussian rigour.

She thought that having kept her nose away from a surgeon’s scalpel communicated her strong personality to the world. Yes, she had a nose, more pre-surgery Sri Devi than Marilyn Monroe, and she wore it with pride, although she quickly tilted her head to offer her more flattering three-quarter face angle as soon as someone started snapping photos. She thought she was doing quite well for a twenty-eight-year-old marketing director with a tidy flat in South Delhi.

Who cares if she was alone? Wasn't everyone, in the end? Anyway, she was not alone tonight. What sort of guy was this one? Her thoughts seemed to melt into the squat, half-empty bottle of coffee-flavoured tequila in front of the two.

'What did you say your name was again?' she provoked him.

He looked at her, uncertain if she was taking the piss.

'Really? Are you serious? You don't remember already?' he asked.

'Yes, I know, I remember your Unique Selling Point, don't worry… "Rusty, single, twenty-three years old, open-minded, and easy to talk to", yes, I am. Serious. Yes. That's me, serious.'

He smirked. She noticed something slightly feminine about his smooth features. Either a high-tech razor eliminating any trace of beard, or reduced levels of testosterone, she thought. Beyond the rotundity of his cheekbones, there was something in his gaze she couldn't quite place. The plucked eyebrows might be overdone. She did not feel 100 per cent sure she wanted to go to bed with this guy, but the alcohol was lowering her expectations. The loneliness … It had been a while and she really could use some release from the constant tensions at work. She loved competition and felt she was born for it, but work felt like being stuck with her power-hungry siblings. She'd tried meditation, yoga, mindfulness, mind training … the whole thing. To calm down. Slow down. Chillax. Oh, how she hated that word. Her effort had resulted in creating a better mask. Underneath she was a bundle of nerves. *Wtf, where's that stupid waiter?*

The bar felt louder than usual. It was another hot, stuffy summer and everything smelled. The carpet reeked of food fumes coming from the restaurant, the couches smelled of sweat, since the owners somehow didn't believe cold AC was cool. How contradictory!

'You seem lost in thought, Sohini,' said Rusty.

'I was just thinking the owners could turn up the AC.'

'People can be cruel,' Rusty said with a neutral expression. Sohini couldn't tell if this was a warning or a complaint. She needed to strategize, now. That was her field. Business Strategy. *I mean, life is strategy*, she thought, *so making money while doing what I already do in life makes total sense … like, why not, right?* Her thinking was definitely not straight, right now.

'Do you miss her?'

'Who?'

'Your mom…'

'Ooh, Rusty, getting very personal on a first date… sneaky!' she chided him but was too tempted to avoid talking about her favourite subject – her pain. 'But the answer is … yes, terribly. I dream of her every night still. I, now, for the first time, not only understand but deeply feel what it means to be alone. My father loves me, I think … but his love is divided between his new wife, who so obviously hates me … how cliché, right? But she does … and my stepbrothers and stepsisters, who I'd say almost entirely despise me, except perhaps for my sister. But fuck 'm. I've got plans and am set to reach my goals. Harder without Ma, true. But she gave me the strength to…'

'Sorry, I just have to go to the loo, forgive me, I'll be right back,' Rusty said.

Odd, she thought. Rude. This was when she decided it would be better to apply some precautions. She got out her phone and googled *'How to stay safe on Tinder in 5 easy steps'*. She ordered another bottle of tequila and started to study her screen.

Number 1. Check your date on social media. She'd done it. Nothing suspicious on his timelines. Photos of his treks in Ladakh, some in a Himachal Pradesh cottage for a few weeks and hiking, friends, family. Nothing suspicious. No girlfriend shots. Smart.

Number 2. Wait before you meet up and exchange a few messages. Get to know each other before you meet. She'd done it. He had good messaging skills, good timing, decent enough humour on screen. Not as much in life, but maybe that's because he was … rusty? *Oh, God I must be drunk to think of such dad puns … That's not me.*

Number 3. Don't share your phone number or personal info, use email. Done. *I think?*

Number 4. Always meet in a public place. Nothing more public than this very public pub. Kinda shitty, really. That's how public it is.

And Number 5. The most important one, number 5. Tell a friend when you plan to meet and at what time. Update her.

She clicked the button on the side of her phone to darken her screen. She studied her nose using the screen as a mirror, tilting her head to catch her better angle. Behind her own reflection she saw Rusty standing behind her, looking at the back of her head. Or was he spying her screen? And how long had he been there?

'Here, I've ordered another bottle,' Sohini said, turning around, as if she'd not noticed him.

'Another bottle?' Rusty said when he came back after too long a break, she thought.

'Well, you were gone so long, I thought I'd take the initiative.'

'Cheers to that!'

After another few shots, and paying the bill, things got blurrier. That was when her judgment got either impaired or refined, and she decided she needed extra proof.

'Look, Rusty, I think things are going well for you tonight, and I'm thinking of inviting you back to my place, but I need extra proof...'

'Of what?' he asked.

'Of who you are. I mean, I checked you out on your socials but still, you know how easy it is to set up a timeline with a different name than yours, right? I mean, I'm sure you are called Rusty. Short for Russell, right?'

'Do you need proof of that?'

'Do you mind? I'm sorry. I like you and, like I said, I think things are going well tonight, but I know that if I didn't ask you, I'd be afraid, one part of me would be more worried. Not that there's anything wrong with you, there isn't. It's just me. I need to be extra sure. I'm covered. I mean, we just met, right? But I'm about to let you into my apartment. So, it's all cool, but ... can I see your driver's licence?'

'Sorry...? What...What if I don't drive?'

'You don't?'

'No, I do. But what if I didn't, right?'

'Well, then we'd have a problem, sorry. Unless you have another piece of reliable picture ID.'

'Lucky for us I do drive, and I just so happen to have my driver's licence on me,' he said, reaching into his pocket and sliding his licence out of a transparent plastic credit-card sized wallet. He held it in his hand, showing it to her from a distance.

'Can I hold it?' she asked.

He handed it over to her.

'Oh, Ritesh. That's your full name. I get it. Ritesh, Rusty. Okay…'

She quickly pulled out her phone and snapped a picture. That was when she wrote the message to her friend, attaching the photo of the driver's licence.

'You know that people can get fake driver's licences, right?' said Rusty Ritesh with an exaggerated grin.

'Oh, yes, I know, but hey…' She was about to say something but had a second thought.

'Okay, should we go?' said Rusty.

'Yes, okay, listen, I must go to the ladies' room, now, so you go ahead and wait for me outside, okay? I'll meet you right out in a moment. Yes, see you in a sec,' Sohini said, heading to the bathroom while Rusty picked up his driver's licence from the table, wiped it clean with a napkin, and threw it in a trash can.

The Hand Sanitizer

KNOCK, KNOCK. THE DOOR. AGAIN. THIS HOUSE SEEMS TO find zero rest. It's a constant symphony of water pumps droning feverishly from below, hammers hitting the scaffolding of a new house adding shadows to the street, the archaic chant of the skinny man on his chariot bicycle screaming for the 'paaapeeeeer' he's come to collect. And now, the daily flow of delivery people. Food delivery, Amazon delivery, Swiggy, Deliveroo, appliance delivery, bread delivery, medicine delivery. If only one could be delivered from delivery.

'Here are madam's car keys,' says Krishna. He's been the family driver for over a year now. He was chattier when he first started. Particularly good spoken English, and quite quick with his smartphone. Told the story of his life in less than five minutes. Left Nepal with his wife eighteen years ago, had been in Bangalore since then. Speaks okay Kannada, but, in Bangalore, English is the main language. It's a city of immigrants. Young immigrants. He came lured by the opportunities offered by the call centres. A polishing school for those who believe in the American dream. But this is still India. Some made it, conquered that step up the ladder. He didn't. And so, he's a driver. His wife makes delicious momos.

You just have to try one and you'll see. All the friends of the family he works for have heard about the famous momos. And they order. He's got entrepreneurial skills. Krishna was lucky he found Unni, who'd been running a taxi service with high ambitions. He's the one who got him jobs. Then 2008 happened. Financial trouble for everyone. But after a while, business picked up again. Then Uber and Lyft and Ola happened and forget it. Better find a good family who needs a driver. Unni went luxury driver and then found this family for his friend Krishna.

As the door opens, Anju sees that Krishna reaches for something on the counter by the side of the garage door. She hears what Krishna tells her but that's not what startles her. She has just come back from the Emirates. It's only a one-and-a-half-hour difference in time zones, but she always feels jet-lagged. She is head of a designer firm in Dubai, which she loves, but always longs for the comfort of home. She's in her early forties now and has come back to stay with her parents for Christmas. She came alone, as her partner had to stay in the Gulf to tie up last-minute business. Or so he said.

She looks at Krishna without saying anything. He stands there with the car keys dangling in the air, not sure what to do, smiling. As if absentminded, it takes Anju a few instants before automatically smiling back with her eyes, the only part of her face one sees, as she always flips on her mask before opening the main door. She notices Krishna is not wearing a mask. But that's not what disconcerts her. It is something more subtle. It's only 11 a.m. It can't be ... She thinks that, maybe, her mask is playing tricks on her olfactory sense. So, she ever so slightly pulls on it to expose her nose. But there it is, as sure as Diwali firecrackers: the distinct, pungent smell of alcohol.

She takes the key and Krishna steps back, turns around and heads to the gate to reach the car parked outside, where he spends most of the day waiting to be summoned to go buy groceries or run errands. No special raise was discussed with him, and yet, he thinks while sitting in the Maruti Suzuki embraced again by the comfortable smell of his own body, he is exposing himself to the viral risk more than anyone else in the family during this pandemic. He is the one going to the Nilgiris supermarket. Madam goes perhaps once every two weeks now, not every other day, as she used to.

Anju stands there at the threshold, still trying to catch a whiff of it. Yes, definitely alcohol. He is reeking of it. Then she thinks about what she noticed earlier in the day. She was standing by the window of her bedroom, on the first floor, above the main door. It had been so convenient for her, the location of her room, so far away from her parents' bedroom. She could come back any time of the night without having to explain anything. Not that her mom or dad ever questioned her schedule. She'd been raised to be independent, to do as she pleased. Even too much, she thought. She wouldn't have minded a bit more butting in. Annoying, but a sign of interest. All this freedom could be mistaken for lack of love, and this is what she suspected, deep down.

She had glanced out the window, attracted by the clanking noise of the yellow gate, when she noticed Krishna. She'd not seen him in over six months, since her last trip to Bangalore. He seemed fatter, slower, complacent. He was opening the gate for the cleaning lady, who waddled in slowly because of a limp caused by an aging hip bone. He had a strange smirk. She had almost not recognized him. He seemed bloated and a bit too slow. He moved like Babu, the driver who had left them after extorting some extra money with a bogus story about losing a wallet while he was on a pilgrimage in a Keralan temple. Babu dragged his feet around like that too. It was never clear if it was over-the-counter tranquillizers or something else that had slowly made him go to seed. Krishna's arrival, with his Northern dynamism and direct approach, had seemed so refreshing.

But now he seems to be a different man, almost too confident in his role. It is clear to her. Long months of idleness, having to leave the house only for errands, not to drive her father to the factory, as it had been shut for the lockdown, must have driven him towards a bad habit. Alcohol.

'Mom, did you smell it too?' she asks as she closes the door and turns around to discover her mother standing behind her, a stern expression on her face.

'Yes, I did,' she says.

At lunchtime, while they are dipping the tip of their fingers in paneer butter masala and paratha, drinking the delicious buttermilk she always misses in Dubai, Anju decides to speak up.

'Daddy, daddy, I'm sorry to say it but I think the driver is drinking on the job.'

Father rolls his eyes and sighs.

'Must be like Babu,' she adds. 'They get bored, and they drink. I mean, nothing wrong if you do it on your free time. I mean, daddy, you like your drink too…'

'He sure does,' her mother says, eyes rolling.

'But at eleven in the morning? This is dangerous. What if you have to be driven somewhere urgently and he's in this state?'

'What should I do?' her father says. He hates having to face another management issue. The machines at the factory keep malfunctioning. The production manager died of a heart attack on the job just two weeks before, and the accountant had been swept away by the virus. The house cars keep getting flat tyres or dead batteries. The fans keep giving up and need the coil replaced. The AC breaks down every two months. The water pipes are too old but you need to take down all the walls to rebuild them, so it's better to live with a little mildew here and there, seasonally, than having to move out for months and have everything rebuilt. The world is unabashedly coming apart on a daily basis. And he has to mend it. That's his job, his role, his constant task. Heck, his office is still filing taxes for his daughter! Not that he minds. He relishes this role. He feels needed, important. Kind of a lifesaver if you've already turned seventy-five, as he has. But he's still so active and alert. In charge. Good food and good genes. And a brisk morning walk of at least an hour. Everyday. But having to find a trusted new driver is something that stresses him out.

'Maybe it was just a once in lifetime mistake?' he tries to wiggle his way out.

'Do you think so?'

'Truth is, Krishna told me he brought his father down from Kathmandu to see what could be done in the hospital here. Father is a drinker, you see. Doctors slit him open, took a look at his liver, patched him back up and said: "There's nothing to do, too late, just wait for death, it will come soon". So, he sent him back to Nepal.'

'You know, one of the things that are definitely inherited from parents is a tendency towards alcoholism,' says Anju, who has read it somewhere online, at some point of her Facebook life.

'I guess I'll have to talk to him ...' Father hates conflict. He is all about harmony. It's always better to solve things by paying them away. But something like this can't be danced around, he thinks.

'Yes, you *will* talk to him,' says mother.

'Okay, I will, I will, but what should I tell him? I will say what you tell me.'

'Say that mom and I smelled a lot of alcohol on him this morning and that it's fine if he drinks in his free time, but not on the job. It is dangerous to himself and to passengers. Not to speak of the Maruti Suzuki. Remember how many cars Babu banged up, with the excuse of traffic in Bangalore?'

'Babu...' Father shudders.

'Yes, Babu. We don't want another one of those, do we?' mother says.

'Okay, you just tell him that. Just say that it's okay, his job is not at risk, but that we smelled it. It's important he understands we are aware of this.'

Later in the afternoon, Anju and her mother are having tea in the veranda when they hear some louder-than-usual tones coming from downstairs. Father and Krishna are speaking in Hindi to each other. Father is repeating almost word for word what he's been told to say. Krishna doesn't sound happy at all. Father emerges from the stairs, flustered.

'He is denying it. Especially since he grew up with a father like that, he doesn't touch the stuff, he said. He said maybe it was his perfume. He just changed it, got it as a gift from Diwali. Made me smell it, but it didn't really smell like booze. Then he said that it's fine anyway because life is getting too expensive in Bangalore, his daughter has to go to a new school and they can't afford the fees, so he was going to quit in March anyway. Wants to go back to Nepal, he said. With the whole family. Wants to be there when his father dies. The momo business is not enough, so … But that's not good, Krishna is such a good driver. Even you approved of him!' father says, pointing to his wife.

'That's true,' Anju says, 'and it's quite hard to get your approval, mom…'

'Yes, he is a very good driver, efficient, reliable, he can use the map on his smartphone, which Babu never did and then we'd always get lost,' mother says.

'Now we will lose him. Which is a real problem because new drivers always want more money. What to do? I don't know if I can afford to pay more than what I'm paying him.'

Half an hour later, Anju's phone rings. It's the other driver, Unni. She has used him to go to the airport in the past. He's calling to vouch for Krishna. He's not a drinker. He is a straight arrow, Unni insists.

'Krishna is quite insulted by the accusation. Could it be something else that you smelled?' Unni asks. 'Could you check your entrance or the garage to see if something there could smell like that?'

Anju hangs up and goes downstairs. She sniffs around the hallway. Nothing. Pristine smell of cleaning products. Then she opens the door to the garage. Krishna had reached for something on the counter by the entrance. She thought it was perhaps a concealed bottle of rum. But when she steps out, while Krishna is shuffling around beyond the yellow gate, fiddling with the hood of the Maruti Suzuki, she notices a large plastic bottle. It is filled with pink liquid. With a little pump on top. She presses it instinctively, a gesture she has made so many times while leaving her building in Dubai, or at any entrance of any shop in any of the many malls she spends her evenings at, surrounded by lonely men wearing long white robes and typing on their phones.

The intense smell of alcohol reaches her nostrils. It's so strong she yanks her chin to the side with a shudder. It's one of those cheap, highly alcoholic solutions used in Bangalore. You can get drunk just with a whiff of this thing, she thinks. She realizes that, as Krishna opened the door immediately after sanitizing his hands, the draft brought into the house the smell from his hands, not from his mouth reeking of moonshine or rum or whatever her imagination had made her think Krishna was drinking.

She is now mortified. And yet, doubt lingers. But more than a doubt it's resistance. Not wanting to be proven so wrong. To have insulted the son of an alcoholic man whose liver is so past cirrhosis that he has been sent home to die alone, as there is nothing else to do for him.

She pulls her mask from her neck, up to her nose and calls for Krishna to come to the door.

'You know, I just used the sanitizer there by the door. It smells intensely of alcohol, Krishna…'

'Yes, that's what it was!' The driver's eyelids lift up to the eyebrows. 'That's it!' he says, without smiling, still hurt by the accusation.

'I was thinking about what you said to my father,' Anju says.

'What?'

'About you wanting to leave because Bangalore is too expensive.'

'Yes.'

'And I thought that if you let me know what the fees for your daughter's new school are, and, if they are within my budget, I would like to personally pay for her school costs for the next four years, or however long. Would that help in keeping you in Bangalore?'

'I will enquire, and I will let you know, madam.'

Anju smiles and says, 'thank you, Krishna', and closes the door seeing Krishna smile back ever so rapidly.

He then turns around to walk towards the yellow gate and under his breath lets out a liberating माँ चिकनी or 'ma-chikne' which can be loosely translated from Nepali as 'you mother fucker'.

The Portrait

The truth is that I always felt uncomfortable about the attraction I felt for my mother's friend Mimma. What I found surprising was that neither of them seemed aware that my enthusiasm for Mimma was not simply that of a friendly son but of someone who felt the magnetism of an attractive woman.

She had indolent green eyes, deep and distant at the same time, and a perfectly straight and well-proportioned nose above lips that were not too full but often poised into a sensual pout. She had a melancholic gaze towards the world, looking at everyone with the irresistible non-attachment of a silent movies' diva. Whenever there was a chance to visit her, I would take it.

She'd been divorced for decades. I cannot remember her with her husband, whom I met only later and under different circumstances. His cheerful optimism and his businessman's vigour seemed to contrast so strongly with Mimma's languor. How could these two have conceived two children, I often asked myself.

I was already in my thirties and Mimma in her mid-fifties when I began to fantasize about her. I felt horribly embarrassed about the Freudian misery of it all. Was it a way to divert my forbidden attraction to my own good-looking mother? Was I that banal in my complex? Nevertheless, this was a physical reaction, and I did not bother repressing it.

Accompanying my mother on her visits, stopping by her house on our way back from a stroll in the countryside, was not enough for me. I had to find a way to see her more often, but I didn't dare being more straightforward. My cowardice grew in the following months, turning into the characterizing trait of my relationship with this family.

Mimma's son, Marco, was the solitary type. An anti-social man my age who had an obsession for guns and art. I presume at the time Mimma thought Marco was slightly on the spectrum of autism. It was much more than that. Mimma had gotten a university degree in psychology, in her late forties, and had begun receiving patients in her large studio, deep in the heart of a top floor apartment with a balcony and a view on the green hills of the narrow valley she lived in.

Her son Marco stuttered, spoke very slowly and always grinned in embarrassment when he was with strangers whose questions he didn't necessarily feel he had to answer. He was prematurely bald, with an impressively bulging forehead, narrow, droopy shoulders, and a generally emaciated and cerulean body. His pallor always made me think of the long afternoons he must've spent in the dark of his bedroom, sinking in a depression that seemed to affect Mimma as well. Or had he inherited it from her?

I had the belief that the few words he uttered were somewhat imbued with deep ancient knowledge. It seemed to me the few things he said could've either been naïve truisms or the most intelligent thoughts I had ever heard.

When I asked him why he had not stayed in the university town where he studied art, instead of returning to this suffocating small town he grew up in, he answered: 'It makes no difference to me.' He struck me as an idiot savant, and yet I was not sure how much of an idiot and how much of a sage he was. Maybe he was the savant and I the idiot for attempting to strike a friendship with him so I could see his mother Mimma.

Marco liked me well enough. He seemed unused to people understanding him. And so, his round, scared eyes became even wider and took on a brighter shine when I walked through the heavy wooden door of their apartment for a visit.

I immediately took a liking to his paintings. He was talented enough. He had excelled in art class during high school, although he had not been able to finish his university degree. Yet he had mastered oil and acrylic techniques and had earned praise from his teachers. Those landscapes depicting obsessive urban landscapes seemed to record the intrinsic sadness of the excesses of drab new buildings that came up in the sixties, beige squarish apartment complexes you could observe across from his studio's window, in that small European town he lived in with his mother.

I would visit him, and we would look at his paintings and discuss them. I was enjoying my role as art critic and encouraging friend who prodded him on by analysing what he was creating, while secretly yearning for Mimma to pop her head into the studio and ask if we wanted tea and cookies. I would then sit in the kitchen and study her every move, enamoured with what looked like, perhaps only to my eyes, her innate grace. I was admiring the beauty of her youth still vibrating below the rigidity of middle age, which was slowly inching into her joints, framing a fixed sad expression on her face.

She was a lethargic type, hated exercise and anything dynamic. She was neither too thin nor too fat. She seemed perfect to me, as I tried to imagine her without that thick cardigan, or without that inelegant long skirt and those shoes that seemed too comfortable to have ever been fashionable.

Marco had just completed a painting that I found was his best work, and that proved to really be his best art in the years to come when things got too complicated in my relationship with his family. The picture had a red background, and it depicted the torso of a young man in bronze hues. It was not a Greek Apollo's build, but the unassuming torso of an artist, an intellectual, perhaps, and it was highly likely it was Marco's chest and stomach. The image was floating in all this red, which was not blood red, nor a dark, gloomy shade of crimson but rather a lighter tone, not cheerful but fresh.

The detail, which somewhat repelled a more traditional gaze, like that of my mother who hated the painting at first sight, was the wrist. All was normal on the left, but the right arm disappeared at the wrist and a right hand was painted floating into the red nothingness, a few centimetres from the cut off wrist.

I told Marco I thought that the right hand detached from the arm represented the artist's frustration with the incapacity to create – a declaration of impotence, which is quite universal. He smiled, looking at the painting, then looked at the floor and smiled some more. I was hypnotized by this painting, and, in a way, I secretly thought it represented my difficulty in taking hold of the situation with his mother, whom I impotently continued to covet.

I suppose I was so enthusiastic in describing what I felt in front of this painting that Marco was quite affected. He decided to gift it to me. I could not accept, I told him. He insisted. I was excited to have this image in my possession, to be able to nail it above my bed and contemplate it as long as I wanted.

After this gift, things changed. Marco had now begun to paint in a different style. He had been deeply obsessed with the work of Francis Bacon and had begun to replicate the out-of-focus, distorted style of the English painter. The problem was that his paintings were just too similar to Bacon's creations.

This imitation game was a generational problem. At the time, I had two friends who were writers. They seemed to both have given up on the concept of originality and had fully embraced the post-modern idea that everything had already been said and thought out better than anyone could say and think – all that was left to do, as an artistic act, was to imitate and recompose what already existed.

One of them was obsessed with the writing of the American novelist Thomas Pynchon and so he changed his legal name to Tommaso Pincio, the Italianized version of that English name. Another was obsessed with the feverish style of the Austrian writer and playwright Thomas Bernhard and only wrote stories and novels with the exact same style of this author, but he set them on the Southern side of the Alps and called his main character Tomas.

Similarly, Marco had decided, or maybe it happened spontaneously, to channel Francis Bacon and began a series of portraits of men in power, like Catholic Popes and Archbishops, or Presidents of the National Bank, or industrialists and magnates. Around them he always painted a straight line to compose what looked like a transparent box, like the bullet-proof protection in the Popemobile. He then disfigured them with an eerie touch of his brush. Just like Francis Bacon. Too much like Francis Bacon to be liked by the critics.

It was while observing one of his latest productions of this plagiaristic period that I finally met Marco's sister, Alessandra. She was a petite, sensitive, ethereal woman seven years younger than Marco and me. She loved to write, mostly obscure and enigmatic poems but also sarcastic short stories. She had a peculiarly soft voice, as if she didn't want to disturb the world, as if she were afraid of the sound of her own throat, that whispered and meowed at the same time.

After meeting her rambunctious and effusive father, I realized that Alessandra lived in fear of his uncontained vitality, which she had inherited but repressed. She was constantly editing herself in order to avoid appearing like him. She looked like him, with a long-puckered mouth which always seemed to be sucking juice through a straw, and the same small, quick eyes, but she had Mimma's nose and a proportioned body, considering her contained height. She was cute, without bordering onto the beautiful.

She seemed to take an immediate liking to me. I had the impression, which she later confirmed, that the first thing she had found attractive in me was the fact that I was sensitive enough to understand her brother and to befriend him. At this point, my longing for their mother Mimma had begun to make me feel quite frustrated. I was starting to realize I would never have the courage to declare myself to her, although, in my exaggerated imagination, I envisioned such a predicament often enough. Yet, I could not act on my impulse and on my attraction, which consequently kept growing. That's why I asked Alessandra, as we were leaving her mother's house at the same time in one of my visits, if she wanted to go and have a hot chocolate with me.

I liked how her eyes smiled when accepting the invitation. She had an exquisite and odd sense of irony, mocking my rude ways which I was never aware of, at the time, although it had been pointed out to me frequently enough. She seemed to have just separated from a complicated and perhaps even violent relationship and I was apparently available, although my mind was occupied by her mother.

Soon enough she invited me to her apartment, which was on the top floor in the downtown area of a bigger city, thirty kilometres away from her mother's town. She was a timid lover at first, slowly beginning to open up to me and becoming more daring and inquisitive. We went on vacation together over Christmas to an Alpine resort, taking saunas and running out semi-naked to roll in the snow.

She said she had frail health. She often shielded herself from the sun, as if light, however weak in that Alpine winter, could be too violent, not only for her eyes, which she often shuttered, even as I approached her for a stolen kiss, but for her whole body.

To this day I cannot tell if Sandra, who asked me to drop the too long 'Alessandra' and soon became Sandrina, was truly frail and sensitive or perhaps she was as sturdy as her father but envisioned herself as being more vulnerable, like Mimma and Marco. Like her mother and brother, she also liked, in the afternoon, to shut herself in a bedroom with curtained windows and lie in bed in the dark. Not necessarily to sleep but simply to recover from the stimuli of a normal life, which she declared she found too challenging and tiring.

I tried not to think about Mimma when I was in bed with her daughter. And I believe I succeeded. Most of the time. It would've been, again, too Freudian. Although I was also conscious of my unconsciousness, if you can believe that. So, I kind of loved her, I guess. And she declared she loved me back. Or at least manifested a very believable devotion. We would speak in rhymes to each other, off and on, having this musical capacity to improvise a dialogue that seemed to fit like a slow kiss. She dragged me to climb across the walls of cemeteries at night, visiting graves in silence and isolation, which she found erotically stimulating. And I just went along with it, trying to understand, thinking it was her concealed death wish which dragged us into places of death.

She saw me as raw material, someone she thought she should educate, as she felt herself to be more learned and erudite, an arrogant legacy from her mother. They both worshipped academic knowledge with the sensual excitement of deranged groupies.

Although we had gone to similar schools getting similar grades, studying literature, philosophy, Latin, and ancient Greek, she felt like she had to bring me back to the importance of knowledge with a capital K. She would gift me collections of poetry or lesser-known novellas of Russian authors that she thought I could learn something from. She would take me to classical music concerts, not knowing I had often frequented them before meeting her. But I was not going to disappoint her. She read critical theory aloud to me, and

I pretended to be surprised by the discovery of something I had digested years before.

Soon enough we found ourselves engaged, not to each other, but to an unspoken reciprocal mission – while she tried to elevate my sensibility and education, feeling she had a better understanding of Greek philosophy, Italian nineteenth-century poetry and ideas of Kierkegaard, I would try to improve her enjoyment of physical life by bringing her on skiing expeditions, mountain hikes, long walks, dinners with loud and brilliant friends, who cooked delicious meals and drank too much wine. We were each other's Pygmalions. Or trying to be.

Over time, she grew uncomfortable with the vigour she had been repressing and was now allowing to flow, so she drove herself forcefully back to her cherished yet artificial melancholia, and I suspected that a mild depression I had been trying to avoid all my life was finding fertile ground in her darkened afternoons and sombre moods.

I was increasingly sad around her, gliding towards a more taciturn state, the corners of my mouth turning down, my eyes losing spark and my eyelids drooping at half-mast, in a mask of 'the blues' I would contemplate with slight dismay in the mirror.

This was when Sandra suggested I ask Marco to paint my portrait. Marco had not been happy about me seeing his sister. He had a very promiscuous relationship with her. As far as I knew, he had never had a girlfriend. From bits and pieces of confessions Sandrina had made to me, I had developed the suspicion that my girlfriend might've – if not slept with him – perhaps sexually pleased her own odd brother in some ways out of charity, piety or perversion.

There had been, at any rate, some unhealthy sort of intimacy between the two of them.

And yet Marco could not stand the artificial ebullience Sandrina affected around him. She suddenly became shrill and optimistic when she entered his studio. As soon as she was around him, she finally acted like her father, something Marco could not stand. He felt treated like a patient, his singularity underlined by all this excessive enthusiasm. Plus, my relationship with his sister had now hijacked from him the only friend he had. I had betrayed him, in his eyes, and it cost him a few months to get over it.

In all this, Mimma seemed to be torn. She seemed happy that Sandrina was with me. She confided to my mother that I would be a positive influence on her daughter, with whom she'd been arguing regularly. And yet she was sad my visits had decreased. When they happened, I was in the compromised role of the daughter's boyfriend, having to take sides with Sandra in family squabbles. I held no hope that Mimma was jealous of her daughter, but could only dream it were so.

I decided I would pay Marco to paint my portrait. It would be my way to compensate for the friendship I had subtracted from him. In those weeks, he had started working on commissioned portraits of businessmen friends of his father. It fit with his project to paint men of power and yet he had to smooth over the Baconesque colours and shadows that pointed towards a contempt for that power, or risk losing customers.

I was open to him having his go at me, with his brush dipped into Francis Bacon's gaze. He asked only for a few recent photographs and some from when I was younger. Then he disappeared into his studio for weeks.

My cohabitation with Sandrina was getting worse. I could feel life being vacuumed out of me by her lunar moods. She rejected joy, more and more. She was seeking sadness, listening to the most lugubrious music, having the most pessimistic conversations about the meaninglessness of life. I felt so distant from her views of what existence was supposed to be. She ascribed this to my superficiality. For her, understanding the sadness of existence, embracing it, refusing to resist the drift towards the feeling of heaviness and despair was the only honest and intelligent way of being. I felt I could not afford it. It was unbearably painful to live that way. If seeking serenity was for imbeciles, so be it. I would embrace my happy idiocy.

One of those dreary days, Marco called. He stuttered that the painting was ready. I could come by and see it. When Sandrina and I arrived at Mimma's house, everything was dark. No one answered the door. We had the keys, but there was no one home. We switched on the light. There seemed to be an unusual disorderly mess in the hallway, but we ignored it and made our way to the studio. And there it was, on a tripod, the portrait Marco had made of me. I was immediately transfixed. He had painted the usual transparent square around the subject, the trademark of his homage to Francis Bacon. The background was a dark bluish-green. In the painting, I was wearing a coat and a jacket, which I only wore on formal occasions. My eyes were staring back at me, clearly well captured. Or so it seemed to me at first. It was a stern gaze. It was the expression I found myself having, during those sad times. My head was even bigger than it normally is, the wide forehead slightly exaggerated, the square shape accentuated by puffy hair, the defects exaggerated instead of painted over, an odd bulge in my frontal lobes which had something familiar but didn't feel entirely representative of my looks. But what impressed me most were the nose and the mouth because…

The house phone rang and Sandrina left the studio to go to the hallway and answer it. I heard her voice from the open door but couldn't make out what she was saying. She was slightly alarmed, but my attention was now captured again by the painting. The nose and mouth of the man portrayed were not exactly faithful to the subject. Marco had managed to paint a subtle mix of his own features and mine and now I realized that even the gaze, which I had at first thought was the best-captured feature, was Marco's gaze. He had skilfully hidden himself inside my face. It was me, but it was also Marco looking back at me through that painting.

The man in the painting did not look like me at that moment, in my mid-thirties, still full of the dynamism and energy I've now lost – it was me in the future, it was myself in the mid-fifties, my age, now, as I write this. And that me from the future was staring back at me.

This painting was a warning, I realized. If I stayed with this family, if I let that Marco grow inside me, this is what I would look like in twenty years' time. The man in the portrait was, at the same time, slightly afraid, untrusting, severe, judgmental, harsh, scared and scary. All in one expression. It was the portrait of an intense and tense person, that combination of Marco and I looking back at me, from the future.

I was not scared. I felt grateful. I took it as a warning from my friend Marco, that odd bird I had originally connected with. He had used his art to tell me something – if I continued in this course of action, with the life I was leading, intertwined with his family, I would begin to look a bit like him, and this is what I would look like in my mid-fifties. It was a reverse Dorian Gray portrait, which instead of capturing in advance all the stress, the frustration, the ageing, and the weight of the obstacles awaiting ahead on the road, it was showing it to me. Now. If I stayed in this situation, if I didn't force a radical change, this funereal, doomed man is who I would become.

Now Sandrina was screaming on the phone, so I left the studio and joined her just in time to hear her hang up. It was her mother calling from the hospital. Marco was in surgery. Just an hour before we got to the house, he had walked into Mimma's bedroom with a rifle which he had pointed towards himself. He was crying, saying things that didn't make sense, Mimma told Sandra. He pointed the rifle to his heart and pulled the trigger. Mimma had the presence of mind of slapping the rifle at the right time and Marco had shot himself through his shoulder. He had survived. He would make it.

Sandrina, for the rest of her not long life, always held it against me that I separated from her right in the middle of this trauma. It wasn't immediate, but over the following weeks I fortunately had to travel for work. It was from a distance that I matured the realization that I just couldn't take it. The image of that portrait kept flashing in my memory. I eventually told her I could not go on with our relationship. And I left.

Soon after, I moved to a bigger city, fell in love with another woman and had a child with her. Sandrina also met someone, a guy from her hometown who came from a rich family of textile industrialists. She had three children with him. Then an aggressive cancer took her, just two years after Mimma, while allegedly washing the windows on her balcony of that fifth-floor apartment, fell to her death. Marco ended up in a mental institution for a while, then was discharged and went back to live in the same apartment.

One day, as I was driving my motorcycle in a busy, damp street, a driver cut in front of me and I fell, dislocating the ulna bone of my left wrist, which had to be put in a cast. Once I got home from the hospital, I stood in front of Marco's two paintings, my portrait, and the red painting.

I noticed that the torso looked not only like Marco's but like mine. It felt like a mirror, my left dislocated wrist perfectly matching the right one in the painting.

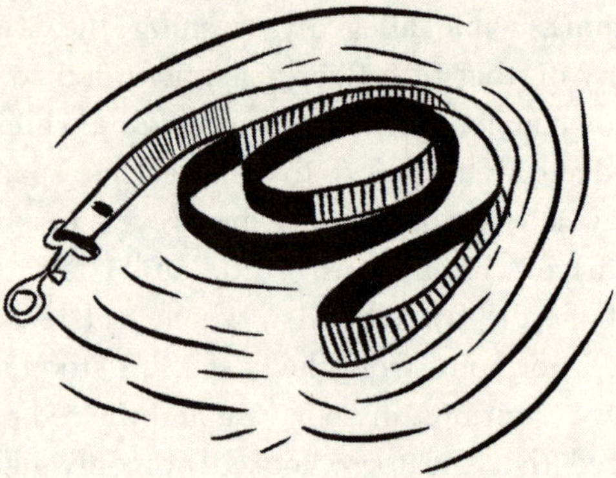

The Leash

'SHUT THE DOOR!' HELEN SCREAMS AT HER GUEST WALKING behind her, in this light-filled house in Hollywood Hills.

'You know ... Ballou ... I told you about my cat Ballou, didn't I?' Helen points at the bulimic furry creature crouched over its bowl, chomping away, not in the least interested in making a run for the door.

'And of course...' Helen looks up at the top of the steep staircase leading to her bedroom where a black furry head appears and vanishes '...Alphonse.'

'Aaaaanthonyyy!' Helen calls out. The house is not that big, so there's no need to scream. It's a twenties single-family wooden house, ready to take on the Big One whenever it'll shake up California, but liable to disappear in the next fire whooping down from the woods. But it also has a large jacuzzi on the deck overlooking the valley, which descends to the city, spreading out all the way to the Pacific Ocean.

The house has three sheds. One stores Helen and Anthony's surfboards, the other is a deposit with tennis racquets, a printer, old files on dusty shelves, junk no one remembers about. The third one is just big enough for a king-size bed, a little bathroom and an outdoor shower and is occasionally used as a guest house.

'How old is Anthony?' asks Gudny, Helen's guest, a sporty Norwegian agent for opera singers whom Helen has met a few times at the local café down the road. They look alike, both with straight blond hair, blue eyes, quick, nervous smiles.

'He'll turn thirty-one this year.'

A bit old to still live with his divorced mom, Gudny thinks but dares not say.

'He's been getting a few jobs,' Helen whispers. 'He wanted to become a shrink at some point, made it to sophomore year in Santa Clara. His girlfriend left him to focus on her modelling career. Now she's a wellness trainer. He had a breakdown. Doctor said PTSD.'

'Post-traumatic stress disorder? Isn't that something that happens to victims of war or airplane disasters?'

Anthony had tried his hand at being a carpenter, Helen says, but didn't show up for work after the third day. The boss just wouldn't listen to his advice, and Anthony knew he could improve their work with his ideas. He then became an apprentice electrician, but that boss fired him because Anthony had insisted on doing things his own way. He went back to coaching tennis part-time, hanging around the courts, asking people who lost their sets, and looked humiliated about it, if they felt like trying to win for a change. But mostly, he used coaching to proselytize his belief that life was love and love was the only important thing he, or anyone else for that matter, must give to the world. By this time, he had decided to fully embrace his half Trinidadian side and, when asked what he believed in, he introduced himself as a Rastafarian.

'Yes, more like a Pastafarian, I said to him,' Helen laughs then puts on a straight face. 'I was trying to dedramatize. He didn't talk to me for two days. Said I didn't take him seriously.'

Anthony walks through the garden, without looking inside the house. Average height, athletic build, small nose. He has grown out his hair long and wild, his beard jutting out like an Egyptian pharaoh's.

'Yeah, I know,' Helen says, 'that hair… He says he doesn't care. He said he learned not to care when he lived on his own for a while.' Anthony, Helen recounts, after a strong disagreement with her, moved out to live in his car for a few weeks. It was kind of a hip thing to do in Southern California. He said he had gotten sick of sleeping too close to the Wi-Fi router in the TV room. He tried to explain to Helen that it was important to get rid of the router, to avoid the dangers of electromagnetic waves. 'They are messing with our minds,' he said. But he had failed to convince her. Helen did not get rid of the router. So, he preferred to shield his brain in the car. Although Helen says, he would sleep in the parking lot of the McDonald's down in the city so he could get a bit of Wi-Fi, just enough to watch videos for free. All those videos, he had told her, were his school. Didn't need to finish university, he'd said. University was so 2010! This is now. Knowledge is at your disposal everywhere. Professors are teaching online and for free, day and night. Why submit yourself to the lies of a university teacher when you have the Internet? Universities try to encage your head. Plus, grades are so nineties! Helen laughs. Anthony spent his days surfing, she says almost proudly, swimming, and coaching tennis. He lived off food stamps and lentils and felt an incredible jolt of freedom with only the occasional tear of sadness when he thought about the girlfriend who left him, especially when he would stalk her Insta-stories and see her smiling with her new boyfriend at Zumba classes.

Then he had gotten sick. Really sick. All kinds of sick. Bone sick. Muscle sick. Nose sick. Throat sick. Fever sick. Maybe because of the McDonald's Wi-Fi? Helen, whom he never called mother, just Helen, reached out to him, found out he wasn't well, offered to take him to the hospital, an idea he hated because they kill you in hospitals. So, she brought him home.

'We have to be careful with the cats,' Helen tells Gudny. 'Always shut the doors behind you. You know … coyotes.'

'Coyotes?' Gudny asks, widening her blue eyes.

'Coyotes. Old Toffee escaped one night a couple of years ago. He hopped on the deck, then on the roof and over the fence. We heard a horrible noise, wild meowing mixed with rabid growling. Found only some traces of blood. Never came back.'

Helen programmed her smartwatch to alert her of telluric waves happening anywhere in the world. That's why she interrupts their chat, suddenly, looks at her wrist and says, 'There have just been three mild tremors near Osaka.' She also has a mass-shootings alert vibrating on her wrist. 'Oh, and they've just killed three high school students in Pensacola, can you believe it?'

Helen tells Gudny she sleeps with a small backpack next to her bed. She goes to fetch it to show her. It's filled with a change of clothes, toothpaste, a disposable phone with a twin SIM card, a fresh laptop constantly backed up, water and dried fruits. She shows her the bicycle she keeps ready in the surf shack.

'If there is a sudden fire, there's zero hope in traffic, you'd get toasted and charred in a sec. I will hop on the saddle with my backpack and get to the water before everyone!'

'What about Ballou and Alphonse?'

'The thought keeps me up at night...' she says, saddened by the question.

Gudny asks to use the bathroom.

'Shut the door behind you!' Helen yells and keeps explaining through the earthquake-proof thin walls. 'Alphonse loves to rip towels apart and thinks that toilet rolls were invented to tempt cats!'

When her guest comes out of the bathroom, shutting the door quickly behind her, Helen walks her out to the wooden deck. Helen takes in the fresh air from the oak tree and pines above her.

'I don't think I'll ever sell this house … Oh, shut the door behind you, quickly!' she screams again. 'All doors have to always be shut, immediately. These cats are so fast, you have no idea. It's for their own good. But they don't know. Aaaanthony! Aaaanthony!' Helen yells toward the guest house, below the deck.

'Did you get my message? Did you?' she yells. No one answers. 'He made me promise I text him when a guest comes. He doesn't like to run into strangers. Once I forgot to tell him the carpenter was coming to fix the doorframe and he almost called the cops on him. He thought it was a burglar. He was so mad at me.'

Anthony's mane of hair briefly appears behind the glare against the windowpane of the guest house. Gudny can only see a comforter rumpled up and empty boxes on the floor. Later, as Helen and Gudny sit in the living room, Anthony walks in, waves hello to the guest but says he prefers not to shake hands and sits down on the sofa, listening to her and Gudny chat.

'Anthony, please, put another log in the stove,' Helen asks, pointing to the small wooden stove by the brick wall.

Anthony looks at his mother, then slowly at the logs by the stove, then looked back at Helen.

'No,' he says.

'No?'

'No.'

'Why? I'm stuck here behind the counter, and I would have to ask Gudny to get up. You are nearer to the stove.'

'I don't feel like it.'

'You don't…'

'It's not in my floo.'

'Your floo…' says Helen.

'Maybe you mean your flow?' says Gudny.

Anthony slowly turns his face to look at the guest, without a hint of a smile.

'I call it my floo. If I don't feel like doing something, I don't do it. I'm incredibly careful about following this personal ethical code. It keeps me in balance. This way I can give more.'

'But you are giving less, surely, right now. What are you giving more of?' Gudny asks.

Anthony again looks at her for a long instant.

'Love. This is what I have to contribute.' He gets up and leaves the house.

'He never got over his girlfriend leaving him…' Helen says. 'Sometimes I think he came back to live here not because he was getting sick, but because of Alphonse.'

'The cat?'

'Yes. It was his girlfriend's cat. They lived together for two months. He was always criticizing her. Wanted her to not do this, not do that. Anyway, they were only twenty-year-olds. Things happen.'

'They sure do. So, this happened ten years ago, the breakup, I mean? Can't he move on?'

'No,' Helen says, and this ended Gudny's visit.

Three weeks later, Gudny runs into Helen again at the café. They walk back to Helen's house, each with a flat white in her hands.

'So, how's Anthony?' Gudny finally asks.

'We had a disagreement, so he won't come in the main house anymore. Anyway, he's farther away from the router there…'

'And he'll get more privacy this way, no?'

'But he took Alphonse with him.'

'Oh.'

'He doesn't let him out, of course, because…'

'Coyotes,' Gudny says.

'Yes. So, it's the two of them in that small box of a room, not really a house. But he's always there. Barely goes out. There, day and night. Sometimes I see him from my bedroom window when I wake up in the middle of the night. His laptop screen is always on. And I see Alphonse's shadow moving about. When we run into each other on the way out, he doesn't say hi.'

'What about cooking?'

'I changed the lock. He goes out or orders in.'

They hear the creaking of a door, below the deck. Helen gets up and runs to the window followed by Gudny. Anthony walks out of his small shack. He's holding something. A leash with Alphonse attached to it. At first, it appears as if the cat doesn't want to move, as if he were embarrassed to be tied at the neck like a dog. Eventually, Alphonse eases out of the door. Anthony walks his cat like a dog. He talks to the animal.

'He said I was a bad influence on Alphonse. That because Alphonse understood that I preferred and overfed Ballou, he suffers and hides in my closet. Anthony says he is retraining Alphonse to enjoy life.'

'On a leash?'

'Yes, you know…'

'Coyotes…' Gudny says. To change the subject, she asks, 'so how are things with men. Any dates?

'Nothing to brag about. I am disappointed. And not in the mood to date. I've made my money as a good real estate investor. I bought this house, my Jaguar, my electric car, I have an apartment I rent out up in San Francisco, plus a couple of small businesses. All for what? I live in the house of my dreams here, with a view. I should be happy. But I thought I was building something for him, so he could have a family and get an easier start in life than I had. I offered him work as a manager in one of my businesses, but he fired two people, got into arguments with the senior manager. Said it wasn't in his floo. I picture him ten years from now, at forty, and I see him in the same situation, with hair that he doesn't wash because shampoo is poison. He says all he needs is the water from the sea, nothing more natural than that. Maybe … but algae in your hair? Sometimes I think this will all end after I'm gone. That this whole philosophy of life is a way to push me away, while still staying here with me. He is stuck. I've kicked him out and taken him back so many times … I can't let him be sick in a car, somewhere in some parking lot … it breaks my heart. Makes me even more anxious than I already am.'

Gudny doesn't know what to say. 'I don't know. I don't have children. It's really hard for me to say anything.' They finish their flat whites and Gudny leaves. Helen goes back to the window and sees Anthony still slowly pacing up and down, whispering something to Alphonse, who seems uncomfortable on that short leash.

That night Helen sleeps unusually well. Her shoulder does not hurt. Her stomach does not grumble. She does not have the bad dreams that frequently haunt her, waking her up in the middle of darkness, screaming. She gets up, goes down the stairs, fills Ballou's litter and goes to the window to look at the deck. She notices something extremely unusual.

The shack door is slightly open. Wide enough for a cat to escape, she immediately thinks. She runs down the wooden staircase to the shack and peeks in, although Anthony has strictly forbidden her from doing that because he says she makes Alphonse anxious with her presence. No one seems to be inside the little shed. For the first time in many years, the bed is made. There is nothing else in there, just the comforter neatly tucked in the corners. The bathroom is also unusually clean. Nothing. Not even a note. Everything gone.

Helen walks slowly back to her house, when she notices, startled, that she has left the front door half open. As she reaches the top of the stairs, she sees something on the threshold of the door. She must've stepped over it in her rush earlier. It is Alphonse's leash. It is holding in place an empty postcard showing a man surfing in Hawaii. Helen suddenly realizes something. She yanks open the door and rushes into the house yelling 'Ballou!'

The Jade Stone

'GUYS! I HAVE SOME NEWS TO SHARE WITH YOU BOTH! ALSO, I need some guidance for the same. Can we FaceTime this weekend?'

The WhatsApp message ends with joined yellow hands.

'Ooh, mystery…' I reply. 'Yes, okay, tomorrow afternoon around 3 or 4 p.m. Indian time'.

'Perfect.' A big red pulsating heart.

Mithu has found success already, and she's only in her early twenties. It happened just a few years ago. Cover interviews on trendy magazines, international prizes, invitations to speak at conventions around the world about the cutting edge of architecture. She's not a young promise; she's already maintaining that promise, asserting her space in a competitive field. She runs ten kilometres every other day, even in the polluted Delhi air.

On the video call, Mithu is excited, wide eyes framed by long, flapping dark eyelashes. 'Guys, I need your advice, okay?'

'Okay,' we say, almost in unison. We're twenty years older than Mithu and often joke about her being our adopted daughter. She says she looks up to us as her #couplegoals but deep down she must think there's something dull and vintage in our marriage. 'I'm finally moving to Berlin!' she says.

'Wow, congratulations, Mithu!' my wife says. Although Mithu would prefer I refer to my wife as 'my partner', so as not to discriminate against any gender.

'Yes, it's hap-pehneeng. I can't believe it! But, no, I can't stand Delhi any longer. The air is really impossible.'

'Where are you now, Mithu? In your apartment? It doesn't look like it…' I ask, pointing to the empty space behind her on the screen.

'No, no, I'm staying with my family these days. I quarantined in my apartment by myself so I could come here without worries. Actually, I realized I had never stayed with them for this long in ages. Yeah, it's been nice. And strange. My mother, for example … she didn't have any reaction when I told her I was moving to another continent. She was, like, 'Ah, okay, good'. And she changed the subject. But I'm going for sure and maybe for good, you know?'

'Might be too early to tell, isn't it?' my wife, whom I should call 'my partner,' says.

'But I already have so many friends in Berlin, colleagues at the architecture studio, designers I met at conventions, and friends I've made on the many trips there. I don't want to say I have more friends over there than here, I guess probably the same number. So, anyway, since you guys have been moving around the world for a lot longer than I have, I wanted to ask you what I should demand in my contract, you know, like insurance, getting more money. I've never negotiated a contract to move to another country.'

I was looking forward to some juicy revelations about her rambunctious love life. But the call seems to be all about business. So, we chat about these mundane subjects, thinking we were wrong in assuming it was a matter of the heart that made Mithu want to get in touch with us so urgently, when she suddenly changes tone, lowering her voice a bit, not smiling any longer.

'There's something else I need to tell you … Remember that a year ago I sent you a photo of that Austrian guy, actually from South Tyrol, in Italy. Remember?'

'Yes, of course we remember,' I say, looking at my wife, who nods and adds: 'Is it all going well?'

'Everything was going well, although we've seen each other only six times in the last year … he's over there in Bozen, south of the Austrian border, and I'm travelling around. We meet in Berlin when I'm there, or in Paris, or Milan or elsewhere. It's been good.'

'So, what happened?'

'The pandemic and all, the distance … Communication was only through this screen, so I don't know…'

'Okay, tell us,' I say, almost impatient now.

'Last week he called to tell me he finally started psychoanalysis. Which I was glad to hear, since I also went into analysis, and it was good for me. He said he told his analyst about me, and the analyst said: "Oh, you must feel lucky to have a beautiful Indian princess waiting for you on the other side of the world ..." I was furious. I asked: "Don't you see anything wrong with this phrase?" He said, "No, I think it was a nice thing to say. What's wrong with this phrase?" And I could not believe it. I mean, he is thirty-seven, I'm now twenty-eight, right, so not that much of a difference. Yet, this conversation brought out an incredible distance, not only physical but mental, cultural, really. So,

I said: "You really don't think there's anything wrong with this phrase?"

"'No," he said, "nothing wrong, it's a compliment". So I told him, "You mean you don't think there's anything wrong in exoticizing and objectifying me like this, like a beautiful Indian princess waiting on the other side of the world? Don't you see how wrong this is? How it doesn't make me feel good at all to be seen as a stereotype, a cartoon character, some exotic image you have in your mind instead of a real person with a real life and real needs and character?" He was shocked. I asked: "How old is your psychoanalyst?" "She's a fifty-five-year-old German woman," he said. "I think you should get a younger analyst," I said, "because obviously this one is a bit too old-style in her mentality and is telling you things that are not really useful." He said he was not going to change psychoanalysts just because I ordered him to."

"'Ordered?" I said. He got really angry. I mean, he's a bit of a square guy. When we were at the very beginning of our relationship, I tried to explain to him that I come with a lot of drama. "Exactly," he said, "I need a bit of drama in my life." Well, okay … I thought about it. And, as the days passed after this conversation about his psychoanalyst, I got angrier. Because I really thought we had a connection. Remember I told you he likes to meditate?'

'No,' I said.

'He does, and he had given me a jade stone a few months ago. That's why he came to India three times. One of those spiritual-tourists-looking-for-themselves type of thing. Yeah, I know … But, anyway, he said that whenever I wanted to get in touch with him, I should just sit in silence in a dark room and try not to think of anything but hold on to that small green jade stone, which fits perfectly between my thumb, index, and ring finger. To me it felt like I was touching him. So, after our disagreement on the phone, I held it and held it. But he never called. Okay, I thought, I must leave him. This isn't working. I got so angry that I smashed the stone into tiny little pieces with a gardening hammer. I put the shreds in an envelope and promised myself I would go to the post office to mail it to him the day after. And then I was going to tell him. Or at least to discuss my intentions of leaving him.'

'And…?'

'Well, the day after I smashed the jade stone, I did receive an email from him. He wrote that I was too much drama for him. And then, I mean, via email, he broke up with me.'

The Smartphone

THIS COTTAGE IN THE SUFFOLK COUNTRYSIDE IS AN impeccable property. I can't be more specific about the location for reasons that will be explained in this story. My wife and I spent such dreamy and idyllic days here.

After we moved here for a brief residency, she started to spontaneously croon the tunes of her teenage years much more often than usual. She was evolving into a happier human being. We cooked, took long walks, worked on our projects, and shopped in the nearby village. It all seemed normal because we were not aware of what was happening to us as we began to busily document our existence on Instagram and followers started to comment with phrases like: 'I want to live your fairy tale life…'

In the beginning, this fed our narcissism and sense of self-assuredness. The number of likes and new followers we were getting got so large that we began to earn good money by simply advertising our lives in the cottage, preparing a vegetable soup or stirring a risotto, making sure the fire didn't die out in the stove, taking pictures of Pig Pig, the black potbellied pig, and of Duck Duck, the white-crested duck, plus the wild cats, the lambs and the whole happy animal farm where we relaxed, watched TV shows and read books and occasionally tried to write.

But we were getting sucked into the need to check how many likes we were getting for the pictures we took of each other on our sunset or dawn walks, because these were the only times we left the cottage, when we could capture the best colours, the reddest reds, the darkest and shiniest hues of black and brown, when we could shine in that golden hue. What was the point of leaving the house if there were no Insta-photos to be taken? We left when the sun was low enough at the horizon to make us look perfect, in that record-breaking, scorching summer that was turning the fields into a dry yellowish shade, making the animals slow down.

We really must've looked perfect because our levels of popularity ascended so rapidly that, instead of writing, as we were supposed to, we spent between 10 a.m. to 5 p.m. checking our accounts, making sure we answered comments, counting the money from ads, curating this unexpected social media celebrity status.

One day, my wife caught me hunched on the side of the bed that received the strongest phone signal, tapping away madly on the screen. She said, 'I think we have a problem…'

'But this is important,' I said, 'I have to do this first thing in the morning, I mean, I have to post this right now, this is the timeframe when we get the most responses, you should know that!'

She sat by me, 'You know, we already have more than ten million followers…'

I kept working on the post. We spent the morning going over offers to become brand ambassadors from expensive firms. This was when we made a mistake. Our friend William, who had a beachfront cottage twenty minutes' drive from the farm, invited us to lunch. We ate a tasty salmon in the small garden overlooking the sea, marvelling at the pristine horizontals of fence, pebble, sea, and sky. Of course, we documented everything, taking pictures of the sweet cottage and the samphire salad, the seagulls, and our feet in the sea. Immediately, our likes and comments plummeted to the lowest levels. We were being abandoned.

Once we got back to the farm, we took photos of the golden hour, my wife pretending to be a shepherdess with the lambs, pictures of me positioned in the limb of a tree with a book, or me pretending to hold a chair up in the air with my index finger while making a surprised face. A tsunami of likes came back to our social media accounts, like a wave of love.

Two months passed. We didn't write anything we were supposed to work on. Traffic insights looked better and better in terms of views, impressions, reach, users' interaction, and discovery metrics. The sponsors were thrilled. We were getting financial stability, but at the same time we realized we were not able to leave the property.

We were trapped by our new life, on this farm, in the middle of the Suffolk countryside, where we had only meant to stay for two weeks, but now couldn't escape because of the wealth generated through our social media.

We were 'alone together' in our virtual unreality, stuck in information anxiety, lost in the shallows of a Technopolis, having lost our battle against the machine, suffocated by our own net delusion. In other words, happy. But not. And as I write this phrase, I'm thinking it would look good on a post with a light blue background. How many likes would it get? Too wordy, perhaps.

My wife and I talked about how we were no longer in control of our lives. One evening, as she lay in the bathtub without her phone, I brought her a glass of red wine and said, 'Isn't it wonderful, just to have this, you and I, and this quiet?' She remembered some of our memorable dinners, back when we were not taking pictures of all the dishes.

'It's as if those people we talked to, the ones we didn't photograph, didn't really exist anymore…' she said.

That's when I understood we were getting distracted from our main purpose and it was time to take a selfie with the wine glasses and the candles in the background. It was a record-breaking shot.

The days stumbled over each other like people at a crossroad looking at their phones. We couldn't stop posting and talking about captions and filters and possible scenarios for photo sequences. We began to stop our ritual of reading by the fire in the evenings, as our minds were so dazed. We were only fit for binge-watching webisodes in bed. We dreamt vividly, always an amalgam of our Instagram photos and TV series. In the mornings, we would wake up and say, 'Good morning, my love,' but we would be looking at our phones as we said this.

Every day, from a nearby property, an elderly lady called Grace came to feed two feral cats who had taken up residence at the farm. She would stop to chat with us about the goings-on of the farm. She always brought treats for everyone – strawberries, homemade fudge, biscuits.

One day, she noticed that Pig Pig wasn't moving. She immediately got one of the farmhands to erect a few planks of wood above the pig to give him some shade. The consensus was that the animal had a stroke. They took turns pouring water into Pig Pig's mouth and feeding him apples. We took pictures.

I asked, 'Have you called a vet yet?'

'Oh, no, you wouldn't want to do that,' Grace said. 'Not yet. They're horribly expensive, and they might want to put him down. We think it would be best to hydrate him and give him a few days to see how he goes.'

'What if he doesn't recover?'

'In that case, there's him,' Grace said, pointing to a man standing a good 300 metres away, on the other side of a fence, by the forest. I couldn't make out his facial features, as he was wearing sunglasses and a military green cap.

'Him?'

'He's a rather good shot. He'd be able to put Pig Pig out of his misery, if necessary. One shot, one kill,' she said, pointing her chin towards the man.

That evening, we tried to find a walk not too far from the farm, which would take us to the wheat fields where the hay bales were stacked as impressive installations. We thought it would make a fine backdrop for portraits and a time-lapse video I had in mind.

We had already boomeranged Pig Pig and Duck Duck; we'd taken pictures near the forties analogical rotary dial phone, next to the artwork and sculptures on the property. My wife did an elaborate ballet sequence on the awfully long picnic table in the fields. We had to keep finding contexts to keep up our likes and earnings.

We left the property and followed a footpath that took us deeper into the forest. A herd of cows stared at us. A sign on the gate read, 'WARNING: BULL IN FIELD,' so we took a smaller path and arrived in an eerie, open space. All the vegetation had been unearthed in a circular opening about ten metres wide. There was just dry soil on the ground. 'Perfect spot to skin and disembowel hunted game,' I remarked as my wife kicked over what looked like a small hipbone in the dirt. We left that round spot with a tickling sensation at the back of our necks.

As I turned around, I noticed the farmer wearing the military cap had appeared at a distance. I waved at him, but he stood there, looking at us, without waving back. We made our way to the cottage.

After it turned dark, we went into the kitchen to rustle up some dinner. We had already spent three-and-a-half months in the cottage. It had been one of the hottest summers on record. The locals seemed to be in a constant state of pleasant shock, a grin on their faces from the extra dose of Vitamin D their DNA was not used to.

There had been talk of climate change, ridiculed by the government that had won the latest election. The big debate, considering the level of heat, was not the damage to the environment, but instead, which party would get the most votes because of climate change.

'What are you thinking about?' my wife asked, as she saw me staring out the window.

'You want the truth?'

'Yes.'

'I was thinking about how the chicken I made yesterday was so tender because I washed it in hot water while massaging it. And that it was a good idea to add a little butter at the end, before squeezing some lemon juice.'

Suddenly, we heard an animal cry coming from out there in the dark. It was quite late, past the golden hour, so we were indoors. Visibility was too low for good Insta-shots, so there was no need to be out.

'It could be one of the lambs,' my wife said.

We had stopped mentioning our voluntary captivity. We'd had a lengthy discussion about leaving. But we were not ready to lose the social media celebrity we had reached in this cottage.

After criticizing all those who had become famous just for posting things, we had become them. And we didn't have the will to go back to being who we were. Now we were them. The people we disdained. The vulgarians we had scoffed at for their lack of talent, who had nothing to offer, who had become famous for just being. And posting about their non-being.

The extra stress was created by the fact that our fame was connected to where we were staying, the White House Farm Artists' Residency, where we had been invited to work. I was meant to finish editing my book and polish some essays, my wife was supposed to produce two poems and interview a Pulitzer Prize winner.

We did none of that, but we were torn about it. It was as if we had demonstrated to ourselves that we were not quite as non-attached as we thought we were. We loved the virtual attention. We lived for it. It was a kind of obsession. Plus, our bank account was growing without much effort – just find the right angle, find the right light, don't grimace. Just be splendid.

'Sounds like something scarier than a lamb,' I said, trying to see if I could make out something in the darkness outside the window.

'Could it be Pig Pig?'

'But he's fully recovered from the heatstroke; you've seen how he puts his snout on the hay bales...'

'We should go and see,' she said.

'Okay,' I said, as she was already by the open door.

'It's dark…' she said.

'Wait, let me get my phone.'

'Oh, no, just leave it here. Just this once. Please…' she said. 'Anyway, it's too dark to take pictures. You know we get such few likes with flash photos.'

'I'm bringing it just to use the torchlight app … Okay?'

'I thought we decided we would try to live more in reality, without having to take pictures of everything all the time,' she said. I pretended to leave it behind but slipped it into my pocket. Soon we were lost in the woods, heading towards the sound.

'What do we do now?' my wife asked.

'Oh, look, good thing I actually did bring my phone by mistake!' I said as I turned on the torch app.

We penetrated deeper into the forest, where we came across a ewe who had broken her leg and was stuck in a fence.

We tried to get her out, but it was difficult. She was scared. We were scared too, as we weren't used to handling animals.

'Why don't you stay here. I'll go find help,' I said, and started walking into the woods towards something that in the distance looked like a light.

As I turned around, I saw my wife's face, now very dimly lit by the edge of the flashlight on my phone.

'Wait!' she shouted, 'you don't know where you're going, I don't know what I'm doing here. We have only one phone with a torch … how is this going to work?'

I turned the flashlight on my face and motioned for her to come where I had reached. She did.

I dropped the phone on the ground once she was in my arms as we hugged intensely.

'We need to escape,' I whispered into her ear as if I were afraid someone, something, could hear me. Maybe the phone?

'But how? And…now?' she whispered back.

'Look,' I pointed towards the light, which could've been a road with passing headlights.

We held hands and walked towards the dark.

The phone lay in the heather, softly illuminating the branches above and the poor bleeding sheep stuck in the fence.

The VHS Tape

WHY DID UNCLE RYAN BUY A GUN? HE SAID IT WAS TO GO shooting at the range. Okay, but why? To blow off steam. But it's actually because he likes to imagine himself as a cop. To man up, as he says. He lives in Germany where he works as an architect in a studio, but he travels back to Pittsburgh to see his mother whenever he gets a chance. He likes being back in his old room, upstairs in a small studio stacked with hundreds of books he's accumulated over a lifetime. It's officially the guest room, but whenever he goes back, he takes out all his paraphernalia, his exotic knives collection, his pictures, his mementos from the different phases of a life of travels. 'It helps me focus,' he says.

Was it necessary, then, to buy that Ruger P38? It was only a few hundred bucks. The gun is small, shiny, easy to conceal. Not great for precision target practice, so it doesn't make sense. But he does go to the range with it. When he comes home, he's energized, and eats his mother's delicious dinner with greater appetite.

Grandma Ruby. He's started to call her that too, now that his four nephews are in their twenties. It has a sweet sound to it. He doesn't think of himself as Uncle Ryan, but for the same reason that mom became Grandma, somehow, he's now Uncle Ryan. With a gun. Of course he didn't tell Grandma Ruby about the Ruger. He keeps it hidden in a nondescript blue backpack whenever he comes back from shooting. He hops up the stairs, three steps at a time, slides the door closed, puts down the stick to block the sliding door and leans below his desk, where he keeps his chest of secrets, locked in a metallic box Grandma bought at IKEA. That's where he keeps the letters from his teenage years. The friend who wrote every week but then stopped being a friend. The girlfriend who loved him so much and wrote in such flowery calligraphy, but then left him to marry a Belgian engineer because she thought Uncle Ryan would never amount to anything. He kept his journals there too. He has stopped writing them now, but for a period of his life, he accumulated neatly organized, leather-bound notebooks with spidery scribbles.

The box is locked. Uncle Ryan gets up and opens the wooden bookshelf's glass door across the room from him. He looks at the books, lined up neatly on the shelf. There, the VHS tape. He thought he was so clever to hide there the keys of the metallic box. The tape's washed-out label, written on with a black Sharpie in capital letters, reads: Sports Illustrated. He keeps that VHS tape at the end of a long row of books. Who would ever look for it, and who would ever extract it from its case, considering there is no VHS player in the house anymore, nor in any house that either he or Grandma Ruby knew?

He unlocks the box, moves aside a few journals and letters, pulls out the plastic case, sticks the Ruger P38 carefully in its spot, and locks the whole thing, putting the keys back in the VHS tape and on the shelf.

It is already time to head back to Germany. The day after, he must get on a flight to Europe. He begins reassembling all his mementos, packing them back in boxes to stuff away in the cupboard before leaving. His room will have a new guest tomorrow. Grandma Ruby, still strong in her mid-seventies, will come up and change the sheets, dust, vacuum, check that the shelves are cleared of Uncle Ryan's hoarding tendencies, which he'd inherited from her, and then welcome Robbie, her oldest grandson, who's due to make it home for dinner.

'How's your skateboarding career going, Robbie?' Uncle Ryan asks at dinner when they are all sitting around the cosy, narrow table in the kitchen.

'Hmm...'

'Hmm-well? Or hmm-crappy?' Uncle Ryan tries to joke.

'Hmm ... Well, I've been busy with work.'

'McDonald's?'

'I know I should have a better job than that, I realize it but...'

'I didn't mean it that way, Robbie, it's perfectly fine to work at McDonald's.'

Robbie goes back to his silence, chewing slowly. He's always the last to finish what's on the plate. He eats stooped over, droopy eyes on his food, slouched shoulders as if he were trying to protect his meal from predators around him. Always hiding behind his curtain of long brown hair. The mild scent of camphor emanates from below the table. He'd hurt his ankle skateboarding. Again.

'Hey, Robbie,' Uncle Ryan tries to get him out of his funk. 'Remember that short story you wrote in elementary school? It was so good. What was the character called?

Malik, yes, Malik. It was like an alter ego. Remember you used to draw a face on your finger and have conversations with him?'

'Hmm … yes … embarrassing…'

'No, no, it was good. I thought there was real talent there.'

'Maybe.'

'Yes, you had great talent, Robbie,' Grandma Ruby interjects.

She's quite involved in the upbringing of her grandchildren, always blaming their shortcomings on her sons-in-law. She never blames her daughters, who live with their families in Philadelphia.

'You were a marvellous soccer player. I still remember how you were dancing around that ball, man, you were quite fast and elegant,' Uncle Ryan says.

'Hmm…' Robbie feels a sharp pain in his knee.

'Come on, don't be humble, you were a star. You got drafted by the Riverhounds juniors, almost made it into the Philadelphia Union.'

'Yeah, almost.'

'Your dad was all in, taking you to practice every day, you were ready for…'

'Yeah … my knee, man.'

Everyone falls silent. As soccer took over Robbie's life, his grades plummeted. It was as if he felt it would be uncool to be the good student he was. He passed anyway because he was so good on the field. He counted on that. So, he let schoolwork go. Then the knee caved. No soccer, bad grades, he lost the admiration of his peers. He locked himself in the room for too long. He lost most of that snotty air of superiority, but some of it lingered, cloaked under a curtain of depression.

'So, how are things at McDonald's?'

'Well, I got transferred to the McDonald's here in Wexford,' he says, explaining why he had arrived with a trolley instead of the usual backpack he'd bring for his long weekends at Grandma's and to see some of the summer friends he'd made over the years.

'You're being promoted, then!' says Uncle Ryan.

'Not really. I mean, I think that when they put me in charge of assembling the burgers. It's a sort of managerial duty, because instead of dealing with one ingredient you're kinda responsible for all the other staff to do their part so the burgers can be ready. But it's not technically managerial and I only get asked occasionally to oversee assembling the burgers so … hmm…'

Uncle Ryan folds early. His flight is at dawn. Robbie sleeps on the couch, ready to move upstairs once he comes back from work. Grandma Ruby is happy to have company, to trade a son for a grandson, although the sight of that stooping skateboarder makes her worry about his future.

Robbie had recently reconnected with the skateboarding crew he hung out with every summer in Pittsburgh. He filled his Instagram with his acrobatic stunts. Slow-motion flights in mid-air, grinding, ollies, the whole shebang. You'd see him under a baseball cap or a wool skullcap to hide a forehead he always felt was too big. His forehead was so big his friends called him eighthead. And so '8head' had become his handle and the tag he'd spray on the walls of the most difficult skating spots.

Hawaiian T-shirts, loose khaki slacks, dark skating sneakers, sometimes showing his skinny bare chest and thin arms. He had an air of coolness about him, a fleeting gaze escaping scrutiny. In those flights up the rails and on the side of cement benches, he was trying to find his balance while learning how to fall. And he kept getting injured. His shins bled, his knees swelled, his ankles couldn't take it any longer. But he kept at it. He felt like a masochist, enjoying the pain his injuries caused. The aches gave him a chance to complain about something tangible and to keep hiding the disappointment he felt towards life for having let him down. Self-punishment? Perhaps. He'd had bigger dreams. He shot videos of his skating flights, 8head raising his arms high like the albatross he read about in a poem at school, long before, a bird so graceful in the sky and so clumsy after landing off the skateboard and slouching off back to work with his 'hmm…' and hums.

That was when the partying started to get more serious. It was as if the daring courage he'd shown on the ramps and on the rails, the lack of fear of hitting your scrotum on metal and cement, of breaking a leg, fissuring a bone, and crushing an elbow translated into a fierce appetite for alcohol, at first, and then all the possible mixes you could think of like MDMA, LSD, coke, ecstasy, all those old-school drugs and then the new ones, with more complicated names, which all sounded like titles of the hard techno songs his friends and he would listen to in clubs and in cars driving home, hoping not to get busted. The Insta-videos documented it all. The bravado … wanting to show the world what he had made of his life.

Until, one night, a couple of years back, when Robbie had come home to Grandma extremely late, very baked, and confused. He lay down in bed in the guest room, upstairs, which he always felt was really Uncle Ryan's room, no matter how carefully his uncle erased signs of his passage. His books, this outmoded symbol of intellectual relevance in an era which could not care less about it all, were a constant reminder of his Uncle's unbearable feeling of superiority. The mementos from a trip to India, the Ganesh miniature, the bust of Julius Caesar when his uncle was having his megalomaniac phase, the photographs he had taken around the world, plastered around the studio, and that big, locked metal box, the Mexican statuettes of terracotta … all this started to swing around the room and take on a life of its own, the Aztec prince and princes having an argument over burritos with a heavy Hispanic accent, Ganesh blowing up to fill the room and stare at him with his paisley-shaped elephant eyes, the books doing a weird militaristic dance off the shelves, heading down the stairs to the beat of martial march…

'Grandmaa … help! Heeelp! I can't breathe! I can't breathe!'

'What! What! What!' Grandma had arrived in her old-fashioned white cotton gown and her woollen socks; eyes still swollen by sleep.

'I am not feeling well, not at all.'

'Oh, Robbie, what's wrong, what's wrong?' She smelled the vodka in the air. 'You're drunk. You're only a bit drunk perhaps…'

'No, Grandma, no, it's something else, I've mixed things up, I can't breathe, I feel like I'm dying, I'm dying Grandma, no, no, call the doctor, call…'

Grandma put on some clothes and drove him to the hospital, where they found a rather messed up mix of chemicals in his blood. They decided to keep him for twenty-four hours under observation. He was back in the guest room in two days. With a new mind. Not an improved one.

He felt he could not think straight anymore. He had to go to therapy. His shrink gave him some pills and three objectives. Get your job back, get a girlfriend and keep a journal. He couldn't write, he couldn't keep a girlfriend, but he got his job back.

He was always tired now. Not too tired to skate. He would go back and slowly gain his skills again. Be 8head again. Rule the ramp. But now they looked at him differently. They laughed at his injuries. And he learned to laugh at himself. A bitter laugh. He was thinking about whether it was all worth it.

Then came Juana. She wasn't that great of a skater. But could hold her own. She was hiding her breasts under loose jumpers, swinging her braids in the air like a helicopter. That was her tag, Chopper. He had a girlfriend. *8head & Chopper.* All he needed, in order to be allowed to get off the meds, now, was to write a journal. He couldn't lie about it. He had to show the shrink.

So, the day after Uncle Ryan left to go back to Germany, he started to look for an empty notebook in the studio, fingering through the shelves of those meaningless books, those allergenic cathedrals of words, when he noticed something at the end of one shelf, behind the glass-window cupboard. It was not a book. It was a strange object he'd never seen before. It looked like a book, but it seemed to be made of plastic. He opened the doors. Pulled out the object. The labels said, 'Sports Illustrated'. He pulled out the plastic box and looked at it. It was a tape. He remembered seeing a video on YouTube about these things called videotapes.

It was a movie perhaps, or a documentary. It said, 'Sports Illustrated.' But you needed a player to watch it. Then he felt something rattling in the empty case. He let the two miniscule metallic things slide out into his hands. Keys. He looked around. The metal box. That was the only thing those keys would fit in. He opened the box. More books, and notebooks. Boring. What a disappointment. He started to read a notebook. More boring notes written in a difficult handwriting, clearly Uncle Ryan's, about some sort of stomach pain he was experiencing in that period of his life. Then some letters. Then another plastic box. But bigger. He slid that out. It was heavy. And unlocked. He unlatched it. A gun. He held it in his hand and looked more closely at it. It had bullets.

The Bench

ANDREA IS BORED OF BEING HERE. HE HAS TRAVELLED TOO much in his long life, considering he started when he was barely a teenager. Almost forty years of travelling. He should be happy to be in Bali during a season when Venice is always so damp and cold. But he's not. It's just too hot on this island and the literary festival was not what he had hoped it would be.

'Yes … Andrea… A … N as in Nancy … D as in Dog … yes, then R as in Robert … E, A!' He must scream to be heard over the loud music from the speakers of a basement hall, below a restaurant where he's come to hear a rapper-slash-poet, an American-slash-Vietnamese, who is also a novelist-slash-activist for the Indonesian-slash-Brazilian forests, and for brown minorities everywhere, for youth, for anger.

'Yes … yes … I know… I know that Andrea is a female name in many countries, but in Italy it is a man's name. The name means 'man' anyway, so I don't know why they use it as a woman's name, really. Yes, I do find it a bit irritating. Does it show?'

His mother is American, but for some reason Andrea picked up a slight English accent during summer school in England, which serves him well in his circle of ataraxic jet-setting friends. Jet-set, is that still a word? Doesn't using this outmoded term already prove that Andrea, at the age of fifty-six, is really in the wrong spot, listening to an angry rap song in some basement with torturous acoustics?

Bang's up there on stage, with his likeable-slash-angry round face, a striking ancient Mayan sculpture of a face, Andrea thinks, with those pouting lips and the intense stare of his dark eyes darting around the room as he sings a song about Bruce Lee, reminding the crowd that 'I risk my life every day here on stage because I risk my reputation and my reputation is my life!'

Bang paces up and down the floor, not really a stage, just the basement of a restaurant, with columns and marble floors, where the terrible sound system reverberates with a dirty crackle, crumpling vowels into consonants. Andrea has a hard time understanding not only what Bang is singing about but also what Nilima is asking him, as he runs his fingers through his long blond-slash-white hair.

'Well, my grandmother comes from an aristocratic family in Venice,' Andrea answers, 'but, you know, we don't like to talk about these kinds of details in Italy, Nilima ... Yes, I did write a novel about the roses in my family garden, true. It's been the book that sold the most, why are you surprised? Maybe in Bangladesh they don't care about roses, what can I say...'

Nilima is a new literary sensation on the glamerati circuit. She comes from a political family in Bangladesh; her uncle was a president, her mother an important minister a few years ago. She's angry and committed and ridiculously photogenic, with long, shiny black hair, strong chin and jaw. True, those incisors may appear slightly too long, but they are mostly hidden by the sensual lips and the attention is magnetized by the intensive stare of eyes underlined by circles she doesn't bother to hide. They give her the gravitas men seek when sporting a beard.

Andrea suspects Nilima is trying to mock him. He is already irritated with the festival organizers. They put him in conversation, again, with some Italian journalist he's known for years. He doesn't like him. He's some Bel Ami, some guy from a little town in a valley up north who had the luck of getting a job in New York and from then on has been able to have a career and some mediocre sort of success. And he pops up everywhere and they always make him interview him on stage, even though it's clear they don't like each other much.

Here comes Sebastian, an established literary legend. A headliner at the festival. He slowly walks his lanky body in, one long step at a time, like an ancient wooden crane trying to besiege a castle. Noticeably tall, long arms and legs, a thick neck on drooping shoulders. And yet he has one of those faces that never age because they never really looked young. He had one of those intrinsically English jaws and long cheeks … He could be a New Wave lead singer from the early eighties, Andrea thinks. And Sebastian was indeed, briefly, in a two-man group with a guitarist called Tristan, at some point.

Sebastian looks over at Andrea, sitting in the back with Nilima, and gives them one of his famous smirks that always seem to be taking the piss out of everything he looks at; a real English bastard, with intelligent blue-green eyes and a long nose. Sebastian looks like he knows he's the last specimen of a better era, venturing into a stupidly dangerous new one.

The English writer sits down on a bench perpendicular to the floor where Bang is still rapping on about his rage and reputation. He looks untouched by all the fuss and waving arms up there on stage. He slowly raises both eyebrows and looks over at Andrea and Nilima again.

He says something to them, but the music is too loud.

'What?' Nilima says.

'I said,' Sebastian raises his voice to be heard, 'am I covering your view?'

'No, no, don't worry,' she answers.

'Are you sure?' Sebastian insists.

'Yes, I'm sure, thank you.'

But Sebastian looks uneasy. He's embarrassed about being so tall and blocking the view of the show. Something in his upbringing pushes him to do something about it. He fidgets and shifts on the bench. He barely knows Nilima; he was introduced to her earlier in the green room, after a panel debate, among the flurry of agents, writers, organizers and moderators running to their sessions. He tries to say something again to Nilima, who can't hear him.

'What? Sorry I can't hear you?' she says, now slightly annoyed. In her eyes, Sebastian represents the hated middle-aged white man who is proud of his country's past, a colonialist past that Nilima finds bloody shameful, not only when it comes to Bangladesh but, really, in the entire worldwide mess it created.

'Are you sure you don't want to trade places?' Sebastian insists.

'No, no, don't worry.'

At this point, Sebastian feels embarrassed to have insisted so much and is overcome by the necessity to blurt out something funny and ironic, a typical English tic, in order to get out of the situation.

'Well, I don't want to block your view, is all I'm saying. But I can't think of any other solution, if you don't want to trade places, short of me leaving … unless you want to come and sit on my lap instead,' he says with a comical grin, tapping both palms of his hands on his thighs.

Nilima's jaw drops, she turns pale, her eyes widen in anger and shock. Did he actually just do that? Did that tall, goofy Englishman ask her to sit on his lap while slapping his big slimy hands on his too-long legs? He did, didn't he?

She's undecided on what to do. She's about to say something but purses her lips and, instead, storms out of the basement while Bang keeps rapping-slash-storytelling.

Andrea looks at Sebastian, who now seems puzzled by Nilima's reaction. The Venetian decides to walk over to the bench and sit next to Sebastian to defuse the situation. He's always despised conflict. He attempts small talk, but he has a hard time understanding anything. Is it time to buy those hearing aids his doctor suggested he should get? No one would be able to notice them under his long blond-and-white hair, he's thinking, as Madhavi, a charming Indian writer of romantic novels, walks in.

'I just saw Nilima run out. She said she's quite angry with you, Sebastian?... What happened?' Andrea explains to Madhavi what happened, so she says to Sebastian: 'Nilima rushed to the restaurant next door, and I think it might be better if we all went to talk to her. You might need to apologize … We've got to defuse this fast.'

'Defuse? Apologize? For what? I was only trying to be gentlemanly by not wanting to cover her view, what the bloody fuck!'

'I think she might've taken it differently,' Madhavi says.

'You think so? Look, I'm just a lower-class bloke and now I must go and apologize to this heiress because she's interpreting a polite gesture of mine as having sexual undertones that were not at all intended? It's insane! She might have a sexist issue with it, but I've got a class issue with this! How about that? This is so humiliating…'

'It might become something bigger than it already is…' Madhavi insists.

Sebastian sits to think about it. He's had a few friends, well, no, acquaintances, okay, people he knows about, or that he's had to deal with, whose careers have been ruined forever by episodes like this one. Does it matter that he had the best intentions and was only trying to be kind? Why does he have to give in to this spoiled, talentless brat who waves a feminist flag under his nose … Because she can, that's why.

So now he starts to worry. Even his own wife might not like this, I mean, she'll take his side, but there could be a doubt, somewhere, that he is one of those men. Which he isn't? Is he? No, no, he isn't.

His famous smirk is gone, and the corners of his mouth are pulling down into a sad grimace, his eyes getting smaller and smaller, his head tilting to the side, his wrist disappearing between his thighs, shoulders slouching. He looks suddenly so tired. No one in the small group is even pretending to listen to Bang, who, out there singing on the marble floor, realizes something is up.

Sebastian gets up and says they should go find her.

They find Nilima sitting by herself at a long wooden table at a restaurant next door, tapping something on her phone. Tweeting about this, thinks Sebastian, who then rushes over to the table, scaring Nilima who looks up from her phone, collects herself, and pretends to be indifferent.

'Listen, Nilima … I don't know how you might have interpreted what I said but I want you to know I'm the least likely person to have wrong intentions and to mean something lewd or offensive when I made that remark. I'm no hashtag me too, I'm a hashtag me neither, if anything, believe me. I only made an innocent quip, in front of everyone, with no intention to offend. But if you have felt offended … which, again, was definitely not my intention … I do apologize to you.'

Nilima doesn't crack the smile everyone was hoping to see. She thinks this is too easy. Apologies are not enough. Saying sorry is not the point. This Englishman doesn't get it. He's just trying to save his skin. The point is that he should never have done it. He doesn't understand why it was wrong.

'Okay … I do accept your apology, but I remain angry at what you've said because I just find it unacceptable, even as a joke,' says Nilima, still furious at him but trying not to show it.

Sebastian sighs loudly, in frustration.

'Well, I don't know what else to say. I have apologized, there was no intention on my part to offend you, so I hope this stops here, and there will be no need to mention it again. Can we agree to that at least?'

Nilima nods reluctantly and goes back to sip her cocktail. Sebastian moves to the far end of the same long table, next to Mahdavi and Andrea, while Bang's stout figure arrives after his concert and creates a buffer between them and Nilima.

'Even the most illustrious career can end on something as silly as this,' says Andrea to fill the gap of silence.

'I really don't know what to add…' says Sebastian. 'This thing has gotten out of hand … You know I wouldn't say anything inappropriate like that. I'm not one of those men. And I also resent having to humiliate myself like this because of a misunderstanding.'

Two beers later, Sebastian leaves the patio and decides to go back to his hotel room.

'And yet…' Andrea says to Madhavi as soon as he's gone, 'I don't know if I would've made that joke.'

'That's my point,' says Nilima, who now rejoins the conversation with Bang. 'If we let it slide like that, it'll never change.'

'On the other hand, if a tall woman covering my view asked me if I wanted to sit on her lap so I can see the concert, I would take it as a flirty joke,' says Andrea.

'Yes, but what is the important difference between a tall woman and a tall man, when you sit on their lap? There is a difference. And you can actually, physically feel that hard difference if you're not careful, right?'

'Yes,' Andrea says.

And then he decides to shut up, thinking he would rather be back in Venice, in his garden, with his roses, away from this new world.

The Teddy Bear

How Nathalie became Kim.

Nathalie was riding the elevator wearing only her pyjamas, clutching a teddy bear under her arm, her long, thin blond hair loose on sporty shoulders, which had straightened during years of riding her horse back at home in France. She had not quite adjusted to New York, so she had asked a friend to leave a bottle of sleeping pills with the doorman.

The elevator stopped on the fourth floor. She immediately felt self-conscious about strangers seeing her in her night clothes and holding her teddy bear. What was she thinking of when she left the house? Doors opened, two boys walked in, only slightly older than her. One was limping; the other was blond, like her. They were speaking French, which is why she decided to pretend nothing was weird about an eighteen-year-old girl in pyjamas with her teddy bear in an elevator in a posh building in Tribeca. She said she was French as well, and, when the boy with the limp asked her what she was doing in the Big Apple, she answered that she was a sophomore studying finance at Columbia University.

'And what are you doing in an elevator, wearing only your PJs at eight in the evening?'

She told them about the pills waiting downstairs. The boy with the limp pressed the STOP button and the cabin jerked to a halt. The young man with the limp said: 'Okay, let me get this straight. You've come all the way from the countryside in the South of France to New York City so you could go to bed at eight o'clock with sleeping pills. And you are eighteen?'

'Yup,' Nathalie said with the smug smile she had inherited from her dad. The boy with the limp pressed the Ground Level button and the elevator started gliding down again. 'Hmm, I think you are investing in the wrong kind of drugs. I have a better idea for you. This is what you are going to do instead. You will go back to your apartment. You will get dressed. You will meet us in the lobby. And then we will give you something to keep you awake, instead of your sleeping pills. See you there!' the boy said, leaving the elevator and walking backwards with his limp while staring at her the whole time.

She pressed the button to get back to her floor. The boy is right, she thought. And I never back down from a dare. I'll show him, she thought as she put on her best evening look, with long boots and all. When she walked out into the hall, the boys were agape at the stunning young blond girl at the end of her teenage years, who walked out as if she owned all the buildings in the borough.

'Wait,' the boy with the limp said, '…and what is your name?'

She told them. 'No, no, that won't work. "Nathalie" is too goody-goody of a name. And too old lady. What's your teddy bear's name?' he asked.

'I call him Little Bear.'

'Boring. My teddy bear was called Kim. So that's your name from tonight. Kim.'

That is how Nathalie became Kim and how, by giving her a new name, the boy with the limp changed her life.

How Gateau got his limp.

Gateau had just turned eighteen when he had a motorcycle accident. A truck in Monaco, where he was from, crushed him under its tyres. He lived in a hospital for a year, on a robust died of morphine. His leg had been completely defleshed. All that was left was the bone tapered with some scarred skin. It looked like a broomstick had been placed between his ankle and knee. After getting out of the hospital he needed to find a substitute for the morphine. The metal of that truck in Monaco had carved him into a new person. The first thing he told his parents once he got home was: 'I will kill myself.' That was when his parents thought that the motorcycle accident had been a suicide attempt. No one knows how he decided to be called Gateau, which means 'cake' in French. People would later debate about the origin of this nickname without ever establishing the truth. Maybe because a sweet little cake was exactly the opposite of what he was. The same way that the shortest and darkest boy in the group was nicknamed 'the Viking'. Most of the friends he made after the accident never found out what Gateau's real name was.

Kim and Gateau became best friends. They spent their nights dancing, high on ecstasy and coke in New York dives like Nell's, MK, The Tunnel, The Limelight, and the Copacabana on the last Thursday of the month when the drag queens came out for their voguing competition. Kim loved to dance for hours, hopping around the floor with her smile and daring gazes, full of energy. Gateau was restless because he had been dumped by his girlfriend, Julia. He wanted to go out every night, all night, meet new acolytes, proselytize his rebellious manifesto, and enrol new troops to their growing tribe of nightcrawlers. But Kim was torn between her newfound exciting freedom and her feeling of duty. She was an only child with a problem: her ageing millionaire father had wanted a boy, so she was doing everything in her power to prove she was just as strong and would be just as successful in her father's field of finance as a boy would've been. She was used to hitting her targets. She'd learned how to do that by going to shoot moles and rats with a .22 rifle roaming with her daddy in his majestic country estate in the South of France, a bull farm for bullfights.

'Just tonight, I beg you.' Gateau was at the door of her apartment. 'If it weren't important, I wouldn't ask. Anyway, finance is just a waste of time, you don't belong to that world, trust me, you are wasting your time and when you realize it, it will be too late.'

She wouldn't have it and held her ground. Even when, after closing the door, she heard him cry, for the first time. She'd never seen him so weak. She opened the door again. 'I have to pass this exam tomorrow. I can't come and blow up my head with you tonight.'

'I swear to you, this is an important night, I beg you, come!' Gateau pleaded.

Kim loved him like a brother, well, more than a brother because, as they told themselves, 'best friends are the brothers you choose'. He made what's boring become magic. But she closed the door. After a minute, she opened it to see him walking slowly to the elevator. 'Gateau, wait!'

'Don't worry, let it go,' Gateau said. 'It's not important, you are right. We will go out another time after your exam, bye.'

Three days after his disappearance, as his friends worried he had killed himself as he had announced he wanted to do so many times, the fire brigade broke into his apartment in the West Village. He wasn't there. No one had any news of him. His powerful parents from Monaco alerted Interpol, thinking they would see him on the marble table of a morgue. Kim was desperate. And feeling guilty, she thought she would use the technique of Gateau's favourite game as a boy, *Dungeons & Dragons*. She had to gather all the information available, ask every single person who knew him or who had seen him. Play detective. She became obsessed. It's all a matter of organizing data, she thought. Piece by piece, asking every single person who knew Gateau, she finally found a punk girl who had spent the last night with him. 'He said he was going to LA to hang with friends,' she said.

Interpol finally intercepted him in Casablanca, in Morocco. He was repatriated to France. 'At danger of suicide'. This is the excuse the police had in order to detain him and bring him back to his parents, even though he was no longer a minor. They sent him to a psychiatric ward, stuffed him with more drugs.

The psychiatrist said, 'If you let this boy free, he will kill himself.' So, the parents sent him to a Swiss clinic. He was discharged after a few months. He had become meaner and radically increased the number of drugs he was taking.

Determined to sink deeper and deeper. He would drag along as many people as possible. And he would apply his *Dungeons & Dragons* skills to this plan.

How Kim's apartment came under police surveillance.

Kim had graduated, left New York City, and moved back to Paris with a high-paying job in a financial firm. She immediately put a rent deposit down for a luxury top-floor apartment in Rue des Cévennes, not too far from her work, and yet in a *quartier* which was obviously bound to become *trés cool.* It offered a view of the city, but of course, not the Eiffel Tower, which was something only tourists and Republicans would care about. Kim had been a conservative, growing up while listening to her father complain about the erosion of French values. Now she was growing into something different. Who would she vote for at the next elections? For no one, it was all bullshit. That was what she was thinking when the doorbell rang.

'Gateau!' she jumped at his neck to hug him tightly. He was in Paris, with no place to stay, ready to party. She asked him to move in. And that was how it started. Gateau began to bring in his new tribe; some of them were friends from the New York days, some from Monaco and some Parisian kids. All they listened to was trance music, convinced that those racing 155 beats per minute put your heart in a transformative state that allowed you to perceive the illusion of reality. But the main jam of that period for them was not a trance hit; it was the song 'Loaded' by Primal Scream, which started with Peter Fonda's speech in the 1966 biker movie *The Wild Angels* when, at a dead biker's funeral, a minister asks, 'Just what is it that you want to do?' and Fonda answers: 'We wanna get loaded, and we wanna have a good time! And that's what we're gonna do! We're gonna have a party!'

It was the song that would open all the raves they had planned. Those days were all about breaking away from family, from the strict and constant need to better yourself according to the usual standards: get a job, buy a house, get richer, have children, seek success through your biting ambitions. The opposite of what Kim had set out to do by going into stock trading, of course. She knew that. But now she saw her job as a way to finance this revolution. And Gateau would fuel it by getting a percentage in drug sales.

It was a regurgitation of the hippie movement from twenty years before. Psychedelic music and drugs made a comeback, with the whole aesthetic of long hair, motorcycles, rebellion – a seventies revival gone rogue. And, of course, at first, it required being rich or being able to mooch off of rich friends. Like Kim. Rich children rebelling against their rich parents. And having a grand time at it.

Kim, Gateau, and the tribe would rent a truck for the weekend, load it with four enormous speakers and a DJ table and head for a remote field, twenty kilometres out of Paris, a different spot every time. Music, LSD, MDMA, ecstasy, hashish, ganja, bonding, dancing, puking. It was all about the tribe, about creating the right vibes with the right people. The main guru of this movement, their intellectual voice, was Terence McKenna, an American ethnobotanist and mystic who advocated the responsible use of naturally occurring psychedelic plants, and, of course, Timothy Leary and his revolutionary theories on the usage of hallucinogenic substances. Nice fantasies, but to put them into practice required stamina and a sharp mind.

'You go and buy the coke,' Gateau would order Willy, the boy with the blond hair who was in the elevator when they first met Kim. 'Boris, you go buy the MDMA. Kim, go get the booze. And you, you stay sober as you'll be the designated driver. Poulet, you will come get the CDs with me. And you, you go get fifty-five strips of one-eighty-gram acid, okay?'

The trance music fans, up until Gateau's arrival in Paris, had been small gangs at war with one another. Stubborn, self-sufficient individualists with zero sense of community, made wicked by the excessive use of drugs. Gateau found the minimum common denominator, made them cooperate, each with a role and a new name, and changed dance history. Then he began to destroy it all.

The apartment in Rue des Cévennes was beginning to get out of control. People sleeping on the floor of the kitchen, the bathroom, all over the living room, even on the balcony in non-stop drug parties. 'Full on' was their war cry. At the same time, Kim made a name for herself in the world of futures trading in Paris, in the long-term prophecies that could make or break a fortune. It's not clear if it was the drugs that fed an already risk-taking personality, but whatever it was, it was working. She would prove to her dad she could build her own fortune and earn her first million before turning thirty. This is what 'Nathalie' had promised him. But 'Kim,' meanwhile, her party side, was partaking of the constant flow of hashish, coke and ecstasy that circulated by the kilos in her apartment. She danced until dawn, laughed, and revelled in the world of high adrenaline.

She would find herself sitting on her own couch next to three boys who were waiting for their turn to buy the drug of their choice. One of them once turned to her and said, 'So, what have you come to buy?' She looked at him, pissed, and lost it: 'This is my apartment, there's my name on the contract. Shit, Gateau! Willy! Boris! Poulet! Enough, if the cops find out, it's me going to jail!' But she always calmed down as they passed her a heavily loaded chillum.

Then, one day, she got a phone call.

'Yes?'

'Is Boris there?'

'This is my private line, in my bedroom, there is no Boris here!' She hung up. The phone rang again. 'Listen, bitch, go to the other room and tell Boris there are two people waiting for him downstairs, they have a contract on him and if he doesn't come to the phone when I call back in five minutes … just go and get him.'

This is when she jumped up on her bed, ran to the other room, grabbed all the boys sleeping, on couches and on the floor, holding their heads up to see which one of them was Boris. Gateau decided Kim and Boris would go out of the fire escape to the roof terrace while he would go downstairs to speak to the guys waiting for Boris. While Kim was holding on to Boris in the cold winter night for two hours, wordlessly, she understood they were close to the end.

A week later, she was sleeping soundly when the doorbell rang. She reached the entry phone. 'Oh, you forgot your blue backpack here, you say. You know it's 4 a.m., right? No, don't bother coming up, I'll throw it to you from the balcony. Yes, eight floors, I know. A breakable smoking pipe and CDs? Well, you better be a good catcher.' Kim went back and started gathering everyone's backpacks, throwing them off the balcony and onto the street, one by one. Then she started kicking everyone awake and dragging them to the door. 'Out, out, out! Enough!'

And yet that was not quite the end. By then everyone had noticed there were cameras outside the main entrance door. Then two plainclothes police agents stopped Willy while he was driving his moped and found his backpack filled with ecstasy and coke. After his arrest, Gateau and the tribe threw yet another party at Rue des Cévennes. It took another episode for Kim to move out of her apartment, change her phone number and go into hiding in London for six months without contacting anyone and finally moving to the UK for a while.

How Raphael became Cocó.

Raphael had earned his nickname in Goa during a forty-eight-hour rave party where he downed so much acid that when a coconut fell from a palm tree, hitting him directly on the skull and breaking it open with a big enough crack that not only could you see blood oozing out but also spot some grey matter, Coconut, aka Cocó, kept dancing until the ambulance arrived. When it got to the party, he refused to leave, so they had to restrain him.

One evening in Paris, Gateau had given Kim an address where she was to meet him. The door was opened by a boy dressed in short pants and a hood, a fluorescent and fashionable (in the eighties) catsuit. 'Let's not judge people by their appearances,' she told him.

'Exactly,' the fluorescent cat said, showing her into the living room where Gateau was preparing the tenth chillum of the afternoon. They became friends but Kim thought nothing of it until she received a strange phone call from Cocó.

'I'm just calling to tell you that we should discuss when we are going to get married.'

'Stop joking, Cocó.'

'I'm serious. You and I should get married next year at the latest, but possibly earlier, so it would be appropriate we discuss the list of people to invite, and our witnesses.'

'You have taken too many drops again, Cocó, I'm not the least bit interested in even going out with you.'

Leaving her office at the investment firm that evening, Kim sensed something was not right. She noticed that the little wooden box she used to stash her ganja, and that she kept in her car, was at the bottom of the building's stairs. In the garage she found Cocó sleeping in her Citroën. She woke him up and kicked him out. Once she got home, she decided to call him. 'We have gotten to the point in which I'm scared of you. If you don't stop this, I swear I'm going to put a contract on you because I don't want to live in fear. Are you getting this?'

Cocó did not answer. The line dropped. The hospital nurses later told Kim he had immediately gone to the kitchen and stabbed himself in the stomach eight times with such deep jabs that they had caused a powerful haemorrhage, bringing him into a coma and to the point of death. This is what made Kim close her apartment and leave her life in Paris behind. She was only twenty-three and could start again. Seven years later, Gateau died in an accident. Maybe he had overdosed while driving in Monaco. Not enough of him was left for a proper autopsy. He had kept the promise he made to his parents when he left the psychiatric ward after Morocco.

Kim made so much money on the financial market that she was able to buy back the real estate property she had grown up in, which had been sold when her father had died. She can still be found, in her mid-fifties, dancing away at the best rave parties in Brazil, Argentina, Greece, Hungary and Italy. She's still stunning, her captivating smile flashing below large glasses, hiding her light blue eyes, still blond, thin, and hopping around the dance floor, carefree. She has the same look she had in that elevator when she got her new life and her new name inspired by a teddy bear.

The Mantelpiece Fish

As Julia is roasting shallots in a wok on the open counter, Marcus is chatting with two invited guests while trying to conceal the fact that he's overly drained of energy from an endless day at work. He puts up a forced smile, straightening his spine and pulling back his shoulders, the way his mother taught him. No one likes a misery guts.

The smoke alarm goes off. Julia yells at Marcus to run to the front door and turn it off. He shuffles out of the living room, opens the fuse box cabinet, jiggles a few switches yet nothing happens.

'Turn it off!' she yells.

'I can't!'

'Just switch off the thingy!'

'I can't, I can't … I'm too short! I can't reach that high!' he screams, blushing.

'Just turn it off!' she insists.

'Don't yell at me! Don't get on my case!' he shouts back, leaving the smoke alarm blasting. He reaches into the refrigerator for ice, throws it in a glass and pours himself a double shot of whisky.

This is when Wilhelmina runs into the room yelling 'Mamaaa!'

Eight years earlier, Julia had decided to go ahead and have a child on her own. The natural father had been a fling, a carnal storm lasting less than your average web series.

She could afford it. Her own father was a man who could only be described as vividly rich. Nothing necessarily filthy in that wealth, but the sheer capacity father had in keeping three ex-wives and two ex-flings financially happy while gifting a house and a trust fund to all his children, made him somewhat of a magnate. He was the there-are-hospitals-named-after-him-in-developing-countries kind of rich.

The self-satisfied grin of Wilhelmina's Grandpa welcomed visitors from a black-and-white photograph on the mantlepiece in Julia's three-storey house in Ladbrook Grove. Next to grandfather chomping on a cigar with a clenched jaw was an object that now threatened Julia's new-found balance in a steady relationship with a reliable boyfriend. Although, she wondered, could she still call him a boyfriend even though he's older than forty? Manfriend? Language hadn't kept up with the changes in society.

This object had recently come swimming into Julia's life, leaving her speechless. When it entered her house, she had stared at it for twenty uninterrupted, silent minutes, taking advantage of the fact that her daughter was sleeping upstairs.

Wilhelmina's real father had been against Julia having an abortion when he heard she got pregnant. She was approaching forty and her interest in the man she secretly referred to as 'the sperm donor' was only related to Wilhelmina's future well-being. She was concerned that her girl might need what is commonly referred to as 'a father figure'. The possibility that the girl's biological father could actually be such a figure was debated within Julia's close circle of friends. He seemed to be nothing more than a jolly, fun, often stoned, failed TV series producer in his early fifties, exactly the type of man Julia had hung out with in the years preceding her motherhood. He was jovial enough at parties, daring and brilliant during the first few minutes of conversation which were filled with his ambitious projects and dreams. A man whose ambitions exceeded his talents, no doubt. He insisted, with his booming voice and from his towering six-foot-three-inch height, that he wanted to be there for the birth. He lasted less than half an hour in the waiting room and later explained to Julia that he just couldn't go through with 'the father figure thing'. He resurfaced when Wilhelmina was nine months old. He repented. 'We should keep the possibility open that we could still have a relationship,' he told Julia, and began to visit regularly. After three months he pulled out again and Julia, who had never received any money from him and did not expect any, gave up.

That was around the time she noticed that her college friend Marcus, whom she invited to one of the many dinners at her three-storey home, might be interested in her as more than a friend. They shared many memories from Cambridge and the ten years after graduating when all social life still revolved around friends from college. Trips to Sardinia, hikes in the Basque Country, parties in Tuscany, swimming in Greece, and many dinners and movies and theatre plays and concerts in London. But never, not even once, had Julia considered Marcus as anything more than a college friend. She simply had never counted on the possibility of even kissing him or hugging him for longer than a few seconds, like her generation of Britons had finally learned to do after centuries of greetings at arm's-length.

Marcus belonged to a category of stiff-upper-lip dinosaurs. It was his mother who had instilled in him such an intense Britishness, or whatever she thought Britishness meant. She had done so out of fear of what Marcus might encounter in life, considering his last name was Patel and his appearance was undoubtedly hybrid, a Gujarati with an English mother and upbringing.

Marcus wore strikingly precise three-piece suits, a semi-military haircut and affected an impeccable diction that placed him among the teaching faculty of the college he never left, in his heart and, evidently, with his body, since he still lived near campus. He had never outgrown those college years, nor his devastating crush on Julia, spying from afar her different affairs with documentary producers, percussionists, nomadic Roma civil rights leaders and the like. Slowly, patiently, with the resilience and drive instilled in him by a demanding mother and racist surrounding, he climbed to the top of his world, becoming a respected and loved, published professor of ophthalmology, marrying another college friend, and fathering two children.

His divorce had not been easy. And he had not yet truly closed the circle, as Marcus' children were still kept in the dark about their father's new fiancée, who they'd always considered a family acquaintance.

After months of clandestine meetings, Julia and Marcus announced to most of their friends their newfound love. He divided his time between the hospital, the college, his first family and then, when he had a weekend or a day free, he hopped on a train and headed into the city to play father to Wilhelmina, and husband to Julia, although they both agreed the intricacies of a new marriage were to be avoided.

They shopped for raw cow's milk and organic tomatoes at the farmers market, played hide-and-seek in the garden and jogged in the park, caught a film or a play and loved each other with passion in the second-floor bedroom facing the dawn light and overlooking a well-tended garden. Finally, everything found its place except for that object on the mantelpiece.

It had been a clear and complete misunderstanding. Julia's favourite activity for years had been to shop for used furniture in antique markets. That's how they had found themselves in front of the sculpture of a fish, debating whether or not to buy it.

The fish had the hypnotizing quality of looking too real. It did not have the colours of a fish lying dead in the polyester boxes of a fishmonger's stand. None of those blue and silver lines one observes once the fish is out of the water. This sculpture had been treated in such a way as to look like a fish swimming in murky waters. The artist had rendered the brownish shade of the scales, and the darker tone of its otherwise expressionless eyes.

To make things eerier, the fish was not straight and stiff as you might imagine a fish ready to be breaded and fried. This one was immortalized while taking a sudden turn. Its tail, fins and gills all seemed to be in motion, capturing an attitude of escape. The realism was bordering on the grotesque.

The sculpture was impaled on a black stick plunged on a square metal base, allowing the fish to be slightly tilted towards the floor, as if it were not only escaping sideways, but also dipping its jaws toward the bottom of a dark green ocean.

'What do you think about this one?' Julia had ironically asked Marcus, whose eyes simply enlarged and became two very round circles of enthusiasm and surprise, in the middle of that market. She had hoped they would both laugh in jest at how horrible it was.

'I absolutely love it!' he exclaimed while holding the sculpture in his arms; first evaluating it with presumed expertise and then clutching it with affection.

'Well, I'm not so sure … how about this one instead?' asked Julia, hoping to distract Marcus with a statuette of a flying goose. Little Wilhelmina disappeared in the crowd and Julia had to run after her while turning her head back towards Marcus and yelling: 'Well, you decide, I better get Wilhelmina! I'll meet you at the car.'

When she saw him arrive with a bundle wrapped in old newspapers, she still had not suspected what had happened. While waiting for him, she'd texted him her feelings about the fish, so she was unsuspecting of the surprise waiting for her at home once she unwrapped the purchase and discovered the horror.

'Marcus…' she called over to him while he was already in the kitchen getting lunch ready. 'Did you get my text when we were leaving the market…?'

'Er … no, I didn't,' he said as he reached for his phone. 'You know, I don't always check … Oh … I see… "hate it, hate it, hate it" … oh, three times … really?'

'Yes, really…'

'But this is a fascinating work of art if you look at it closely,' Marcus insisted, while slowly placing it on the mantelpiece right next to Grandpa's photograph with the cigar. 'It's really true to life, four-dimensional, don't you see it?'

'Yes, almost too much, though. Would you want a real dead fish on your mantelpiece?'

'But did you know it's made of bronze and seaweed?' Marcus asked with an elated smile.

From that day on, Julia interrogated every single house guest and visitor about their opinion of the fish, in the hope of gathering enough votes for the expulsion of that aesthetic crime she had allowed in her otherwise perfectly original, charming, *Architectural Digest* beauty of a house.

And yet, that monstrous sea creature stared at her from the mantelpiece, as Marcus had made it clear that, since they were living together, he should be allowed to have something to his liking, even if it was not what Julia would've picked.

'Although you actually did pick it,' he specified, looking at the sculpture and moving the pedestal to align it with the mantelpiece edge.

Julia just stared at the fish for an awfully long time, without saying anything.

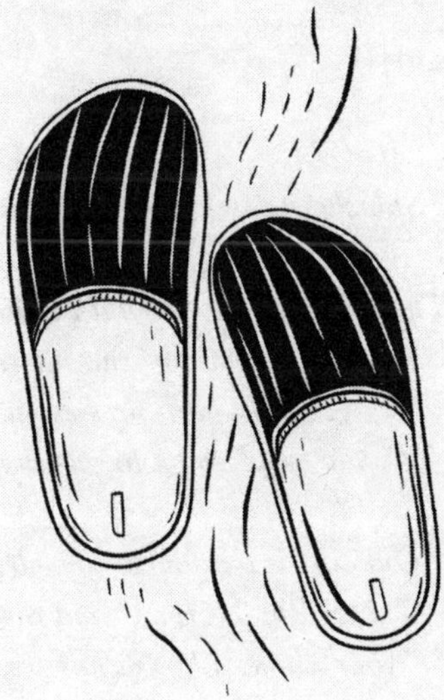

The Slippers

Splashes of seawater (on the deck)
is drying on our skin.
The day is glittering with crystal salt,
Salt of misbehavior and misreading.
A slight pain presses on,
As you bend down to wet my salt.

Our salt is too warm to be let dry,
I scream out the C and the O
of your name. The sea has sea foams,
As the slight pain lingers on

– Filipino poet Maningning C. Miclat
15 September 1999

TWO PEACH-COLOURED SLIPPERS WITH AN ALMOST INVISIBLE gold thread around the edges have been abandoned on the roof of the Literature Department. There's a small petal next to them, still not blown away by the September breeze, which is finally refreshing Manila.

This is the end of a story that begins down by the city harbour, where four years earlier, a ship is about to take to the seas. It's the MV *Greenpeace.* Aboard there is a Russian man called Boris, a Tahitian, a New Zealander and three reporters – one from the Philippines, one from Switzerland and one from the UK – along with eco-militants from sixteen different countries. The vessel is going to embark on a perilous voyage. Pirates still infest the waters between Manila and the port of destination, Shanghai, where this ship is not at all welcome. Its mission is to protest Chinese nuclear testing in the Lop Nor desert. It is 1995 and environmentalism is mobilizing masses in Germany to boycott Shell for having polluted the Baltic Sea with the Brent Spar oil rig; the French President is being criticized worldwide for nuclear testing in the Polynesian atoll of Mururoa; and everyone still remembers the Chernobyl catastrophe, which happened only ten years before. So, there's a lot of media attention on this new Greenpeace mission.

The Mandarin Chinese translator, Ning, is twenty-four years old, a lean Filipino with delicate features and a shy yet wide smile. She's wearing an elegant Chinese jacket buttoned all the way up the neck. The Swiss reporter, Marco, who's just short of turning thirty, has an interesting, messy mop of black curls on a large head. He always wears a white linen shirt, which he thinks makes him look more like a journalist in the tropics. Ning notices him chewing gum with a gracelessly wide-open mouth, standing by the side of an eco-protest in Manila. There's something almost vulgar and arrogant in the way he chews, and his eyes seem a bit too close to each other.

Ning was born in Beijing, where her Filipino parents were in exile, having had to escape political persecution in the Philippines. She returned to Manila at eleven but was in China in her formative years, so she feels Mandarin is her second mother tongue. She mastered it and published her first collection of poetry in Mandarin Chinese and translated it into Tagalog. She's even written a poem to defend the protestors in Tiananmen Square.

Ning tells Marco about growing up in the Forbidden City in the seventies. She often played with a young friend there; a lovely Italian boy called Gustavo, probably the son of an embassy clerk. She sometimes calls Marco by that name to remind herself of her young playdate in Beijing.

On the long voyage towards Shanghai, Ning often sits aside with Marco. She tells him that discoveries often happen by chance and proceeds to explain how tea was discovered, with her twangy, sweet voice. It's a tale of a Chinese emperor, Chen-Nung, who was so serious about his health that he only drank boiled water and one day, in the year 2737 BCE, as he was resting under the shadow of a tree, something happened. "It was windy, just like today in this ship. And some leaves falling from the branches flew into the emperor's bowl. He drank it and was overtaken by a feeling of well-being. And that's how tea was invented."

Marco then tells her that when Emperor Karl fell from a horse in what is now the Czech Republic, he felt that the water of the puddle was warm and that's how he discovered the thermal waters of Karlsbad, the bath of Emperor Karl. So, she now starts calling him Emperor Karl, and he calls her the Tea Empress.

When she goes back to her bunk bed in the cabin she shares with Cory, a cheerful Filipino reporter for Agence France-Presse, and with Fiona, the blond Brit with the constant polite grin on her face, Ning starts drawing Marco when he is asleep, his thick curls fading into clouds in the sky. She dreams of kissing him and that same evening, after everyone has had dinner, and Boris is playing Russian songs on his guitar to entertain all those European peace-warriors on board, Marco and Ning sneak out to the deck.

The sky is just one immense starry caress to the eyes. The sea is shining with astral light and plankton. The wind feels comfortably warm. So, what else can they do but kiss, hiding between the Zodiac rubber dinghies used to block whaling ships in Japan and Norway. Above their head, there is a painted dolphin jumping through a rainbow. Ning and Marco don't know that the crew calls the MV *Greenpeace* by the less poetic name of Black Pig, because of its large size.

Shanghai is getting closer. But Marco and Ning are also thinking of getting closer to each other. But when can they explore their bodies without the impediment of clothes? Not on the deck. Too risky. And messy. Ning has never done it, so it should be in a proper bed. At least for the first time. They decide to meet in her cabin, which she shares with Fiona and Cory. It will be tomorrow afternoon, they tell each other.

The morning after, they discover that the MV *Greenpeace* has already reached the international waters outside Shanghai. All militants spring into action. They've been training in the Hamburg camp for passive resistance techniques. Some are now repeating, as if it were a holy prayer, the phrases they want to say to the Chinese officers who will arrest them. They are preparing signs that read: 'Save the environment' and 'Stop Chinese nuclear testing'.

Marco and Ning confess their worries to each other. Beijing has promised to jail anyone entering its borders without authorization and reminded world media that the penalty for everyone, not just militants but also collaborators, such as translators or journalists, is ten years in jail for counter-revolutionary activities.

Nonetheless, as the Black Pig reaches the mouth of the Yangtze river, the Swedish captain decides to enter Chinese territorial waters, unauthorized to do so by the repeated warnings of the harbour authority coming over the radio.

'We are coming. We have a message we would like to deliver in person to Chinese authorities,' Captain Uif insists over the radio.

'Turn back. Return to international waters,' is what the Coast Guard yells back.

The ship is already six nautical miles into the harbour. All Marco and Ning are able to see in the thick fog are small fishing boats. No sign of the Coast Guard. Unusual. Scary.

There's a creepy silence surrounding the MV *Greenpeace*. Suddenly, the militants and journalists find themselves surrounded by six coastguard ships. The officer in charge asks to board the ship. The captain turns off the engine.

It's not scary, at first. The seventy Chinese Navy officers and harbour officials are smiling and polite. Yet, as they realize the captain has no immediate intention of turning around but persists in wanting to reach the harbour, they begin to confiscate cameras and to act more rudely. The thirty militants and crew repeat their message against nuclear testing, which Ning translates into Mandarin. She reads aloud a written statement by the militants. Marco is in awe of Ning's calm in the storm, although he notices her hand slightly trembling as she reads the message in Chinese.

This is when Captain Uif realizes there's no need to take any more chances. Greenpeace has videos and photos of the Coast Guard being arraigned by the militants; the story is done, no need to go to jail in a country like China in 1996. The MV *Greenpeace* takes off again, heading for Hong Kong harbour, escorted by eight Chinese vessels and two gunboats.

Marco, Cory and Fiona are now busy filing their stories. There's a special euphoria in the air that night at dinner. The Tahitian militant sings a melancholic and dreamy song about nature.

Marco and Ning sneak out again to the deck to chat and tease each other and share more stories. Marco notices how Ning has the sharp capacity to destroy anyone she talks about, including him, by simply describing them and their limits with lucid honesty, yet avoiding the traps of bitterness. Everything they talk about becomes a game. And Marco feels like he's almost able to keep up with her quick wit.

They decided to meet again the day after, mid-afternoon, in her cabin. Cory and Fiona are still busy below deck filing news stories; Marco has already sent his to the newspaper in Switzerland. There's no one in the cabin as the two of them climb into Ning's top bunk and shut the door. She's tense but eager. He's careful and takes things slowly. And yet, when it comes to it, they can't do it. It is physically impossible. She's completely blocked. Impenetrable. She wants to, but her body won't open up. They try a few times. He's afraid to hurt her. It can't happen. They hear noises and pull their shorts back on.

The evening after, they land in Hong Kong. They've kept their kisses and meetings secret from everyone. They tell each other they'll say goodbye tomorrow at the airport when he'll fly back to Zurich, and she'll go back to Manila. As Ning is taken to a van with the *Greenpeace* crew, the reporters Cory, Fiona and Marco are put in another taxi since they are staying at the same hotel.

Cory has been to Hong Kong before and, once they reach the lobby, she asks Marco where he's having dinner. She takes him to a Mongolian restaurant. They drink. A lot. She's fun, Marco thinks. They end up dancing in two or three clubs till extremely late. Now happily drunk, charged with the energy of two weeks at sea, Marco and Cory have sex all night until it's time to go to the airport.

Once he's back in the newsroom in Switzerland, two weeks later, Marco gets a letter from Ning. She writes again and again. He only answers sporadically. He feels guilty about what happened with Cory and also feels the impossibility of the distance – he, with his life in Zurich, now so far away from a ship in the Pacific Ocean, and Ning, who is beginning to teach at the University of the Philippines, painting, working on a second collection of poetry. But the correspondence continues for four years. She sends him her poems. One is dedicated to him, and it's called 'The Last Letter':

Alone in my room
one late afternoon,
I seized your letter
and began to tear it.

Small pieces of paper
liberating themselves
from the five sentences
you repeated, over

and over again to fill
a huge sheet of paper
and your stick drawing
of a big shark in the sea.

Upon freeing themselves
from the whole,
the pieces of paper
began to grow wings:

They are the fireflies
of a forest. Each, carrying
a teardrop of separation,
flapping their wings in silence.

Each, holding a nugget
of good thought. Shining
weightlessly under a huge
shade of neem tree

The last letter you sent me
wound up in little pieces,
grew wings and surrounded me
one late afternoon.

And then, they all escaped
the humidity of my room.
They all fled from my window,
all of them, including the envelope.

In one letter, Ning says she found out from someone about that last night Marco spent with Cory. She says she'd been right all along in nicknaming him the shark when they were on the MV *Greenpeace*. But she keeps writing. Now the letters describe what seem to Marco an unfounded fear of being chased by Chinese agents, about mysterious censorship against her, of her fear of being misunderstood by everyone, and manipulated. Her letters grow with feelings of loss and nostalgia. It's too much for Marco, so he doesn't answer. She mails him her newly published collection of poems, earmarking the ones where she mentions him indirectly.

There's a handwritten dedication at the end of the book.

Why don't you come and visit me (cut
my throat, open me up, break my bones
– and see if my marrow has substance
and my flesh is clean!)?
Just kill me!
Ning

He finds it eerie but thinks nothing more of it. Five years have gone since those kisses on the deck under the painted dolphin and the stars. He's amused by the memory but also unsettled. Then the letters from Ning suddenly stop.

A few months go by, then Marco gets an email from a Greenpeace volunteer he had met in the Manila harbour before leaving on the MV *Greenpeace*. She asks if Marco knows what happened to Ning. He writes back saying he has not heard from her in a while. The volunteer sends Marco a link to an article from the university newspaper.

It says that Ning, the prize-winning artist, poet, and art teacher at the university, on 29 September, walked up to the roof on the seventh floor of the Literature Department building. She stood on the edge of the roof, her back facing the void, her arms clutching a handful of petals, like pieces of a shredded letter. She took off her pair of peach-coloured slippers, with an almost invisible gold thread around the edges, and left them there, pointing away from the drop.

She let herself fall backwards, opening her arms, looking at the sky and at the petals falling slowly, high above her.

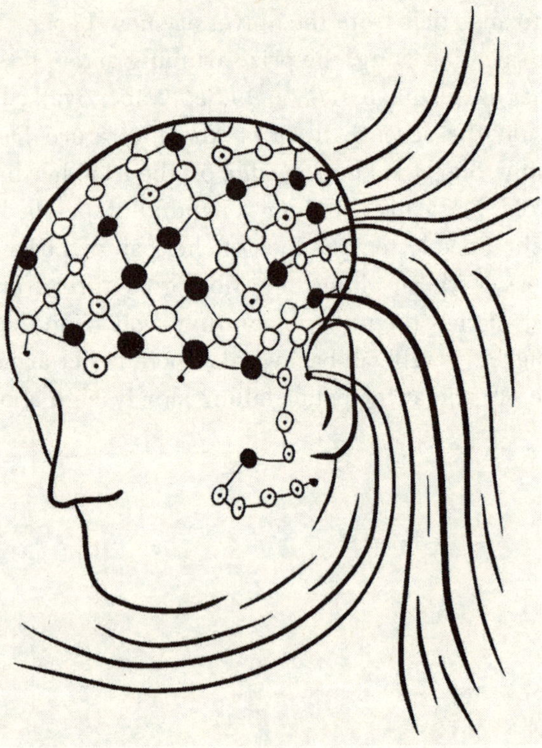

The Sensors

'REMEMBER THAT PLACE ON THE FIFTH FLOOR, BEFORE MY parents bought the house with the pool? When I was eight, it got to the point when I found myself standing by the window, my forehead pressed to the glass, and wanting to jump.'

'Why didn't you tell your mom and dad about what was happening to you?'

'Are you kidding? Don't you remember how he insisted on me becoming a linebacker?'

'Oh, man, yes, I tried to tell him that it might not have really been your sport.'

'It was not.'

'It was what your father wanted to play in high school instead of basketball. Not you. But you had such a stout build, at the time. Before you became lean, like this…'

'Stout? He told me I was fat. All the time. Screamed it at me in an airport when I was late getting to the gate. In front of everyone. I was so humiliated. Shattered.'

'He loves you, David. He was so proud of your performance in the theatre. Remember when we came to see you when you were, what, fourteen? You can't say he wasn't supportive of your passion for ballet.'

'Yes. He let me dance. But all the gay jokes?'

'For people with our background it's not surprising. We know it's wrong, now. But it takes some tolerance towards the past, however wrong it is. We grew up with constant jokes about this being so gay and that being so gay. Heck, your grandfather slapped my hand because I was letting it dangle in the air with a soft wrist. Not manly enough! He was so scared of effeminate behaviour … maybe he had some repressed needs he never confronted.'

'And you, I always wondered about you, Uncle Andrew…'

'I always knew you were how you are. I tried, respectfully and with tact, to tell your father. But, well, you don't want to hear certain truths, even from your older brother.'

'I meant, what about your own tendencies?'

'Look, I've always been around gay friends, whether I knew it or not. The boy sitting next to me in high school, Peter, who studied and partied with me, was always jumpy, funny and with sweaty hands. We laughed a lot. Years later, he came out of the closet, as we used to say. My college roommate came out to me after graduating. My gaydar has always been on off mode. But I have been supportive and in favour of equal rights …'

'I meant, what about you, uncle, you.'

'Ah … well … I always thought that if I were able to sleep with men as well as with women, my chances of getting laid would immediately double. Unfortunately for me, the idea of another man's penis doesn't excite me – quite the contrary. And if I think of the smell, I'm a bit disgusted but that doesn't mean I judge men who like other men's bodies and enjoy them sexually. It's like believing in God. Either you have faith, or you don't. And I don't. My gay friends put me in a category they call hetero-lost – lost to the heterosexual world.'

'Maybe you just don't know. As for me, I was quite sure from early on I preferred men.'

'I could tell, but I couldn't talk to you about it. You were so secretive and distant.'

'I was in pain. You hetero-losts called it transsexualism or even transgender. It's called gender dysphoria.'

'Why haven't you told mom and dad?'

'I have.'

'You have? And how did that go?'

'We were talking about civil rights and equality. The conversation veered to gay rights, and I just couldn't hold it, couldn't fake it any longer. Perhaps it was the appetite suppressant drugs I was taking. I was irreverent, jumpy. Mom said: "Why do you care so much about any of that stuff, anyway? What does it have to do with us?" So, scared shitless, I blurted out, before I could censor myself – "Because *I'm* fucking gay, mom!"'

'Oh, man, and what happened?'

'Dad froze and didn't say anything. Mom seemed calm and said, "Well, I think you should go back home now".'

'No! Are you sure she said that?'

'Yes.'

'What did you do?'

'Nothing. I left. I went back to the dorm in Stanford.'

'This can't be, it's 2021 and this is California. How can this still be happening?'

'It is happening. You don't know how many gay jokes I've had to put up with from my father. Oh, this is so gay, that shirt is too gay, gay this gay that. Zero clue.'

'I've talked to your dad about this years ago and ... It was at the time of your ballet. I said your passion for ballet might be an obvious sign of your sexual orientation, not that a boy liking ballet has to be gay.'

'What did dad say?'

'He said he is a libertarian. He believes in the individual freedom of doing what you want and what you believe in and being who you are.'

'He's also a Christian, and some Christians really have a problem with this particular freedom.'

'He told me: "If this is what it turns out that he is, I'm fine with it. That is what he is and who he is. I accept it. I won't be against it" …'

David fell silent and looked at Andrew for a long time. His dark eyes were becoming glossier. From that chubby boy with back-turned knees, he had sculpted himself into a handsome twenty-two-year-old man.

'Dad never told me this ... He just told me I was fat and tried to make me into something I'm not. God, I hated it. I was so in conflict with my body, developed this eating disorder, but this is so much deeper than just the body and yet it's all about the body.'

'What did Nora say after you came out to them?'

'Mom? Nothing. We're all pretending it didn't happen. We don't talk about it. I think they are hoping we can all act like it was a misunderstanding.'

'But now you know your father is okay with it.'

'Not sure. And mother…'

'Maybe she has a religious problem with this.'

'Maybe … I don't know. It's difficult for me to talk about her … We're close, but … It's dad who has made it so difficult; he's been so harsh.'

'Tell them more directly. Make them understand the silence is hurting you.'

'I can't tell them all that I am, all that I've done … I've gone all out, maybe because I had to hide for so long.'

'I follow you on Instagram. I know.'

'I've taken down all those old photos.'

'It was last year.'

'That's old!'

'There's still one of you with a thick chain wrapped twice around your neck and a big lock…'

'You like that one, huh? It's just playing … and my way to tell the world what I am. I've blocked mom and dad, anyway.'

'I can talk to them if you want.'

'But it wouldn't be the same, would it? They will just hate you for butting in. I just want to focus on studying now.'

David told his uncle about his studies, which, he explained, were about the fact that it is all changing; who we think we are, how we tell each other about ourselves, how we are, the tools we use, and dance itself, his passion.

'What's the point of seeing a human body move on stage or in a street? Aren't we tired of celebrating ourselves? People in cities have been moving to the rhythm of machines for more than 150 years. And now … Now something else is changing … movement, body, dance, all that's changing.'

'I don't understand.'

'You'd have to see it. Come to our theatre in San Francisco in two months. You'll understand.'

Two months later, Andrew found himself in a theatre in downtown San Francisco. It was one of those charmless industrial buildings with ample room for good lighting but poor seating in makeshift benches occupying half of the wide room. He met his brother Harvey with his wife Nora on the sidewalk outside the theatre. He tried to probe him to see if David had made progress with them. Andrew was happy to see his younger brother, towards whom he felt protective tendencies that blossomed when their father died when Harvey was twenty-one and Andrew twenty-seven. Although he tried to like Nora, he felt uneasy around her. She was obsessively protective of her children and wasn't happy about Andrew's newly developed friendship with her son David. She suspected this was behind David's recent outburst about being gay.

At the entrance of the theatre, they were handed a complicated series of sensors. They were instructed to wear a headband and a chest band both connected to wrist braces and strong suction caps to be applied to their forearms. All the colourful wires – red for the chest, blue for the head and green for wrists and arms – were gathered in a single AUX pin jack they were instructed to plug into a hole, which appeared near each seat on the benches.

The three of them, along with the rest of the audience, followed instructions. As soon as they found themselves all plugged in, the entire theatre plunged into complete darkness.

No music, no sound. After the last whispers died out, a feeble light came on at the centre of the stage, where David was standing in a very thin loincloth that exposed to the world the chiselled beauty of his young body. He was also wearing a contraption like the one the audience was wearing and a fly mike on the side of his jaw.

'Our bodies are being surpassed. We can make them as resistant as we can to the dictates of time. But they are bound to fall once, never to get up again. We are leaves, not trees. But the technology we invented is like trees as it is constantly updating at faster paces. What machines can't replicate yet are our emotions. We are still able to make emotions out of data – our memories. Until now, there's a science perfecting this craft. It is called art. We can paint or sculpt a figure, a scene, we can write a story, dance a movement. We can capture a concept into a performance. Or into an object. But all this is over too. We have changed. We have new tools. We are renewed through these tools. The final goal is to transmit our emotions. We don't need a story, a figure, a concept. We can do it with the flick of a switch.'

When David pronounced this last word, 'switch', a faint orange light came on next to the holes where the audience had plugged the pin jacks. Suddenly, Andrew, sitting there in the dark next to his brother, felt excited, his heartbeat increased, he was sweating slightly, even. He felt all the typical symptoms he experienced when he was forced to give a lecture in front of a crowd larger than his class of fifteen students.

'Now you are feeling what I'm feeling,' David said, there on the stage, under that single spotlight.

'I will tell you, without telling you, a story.' And David fell silent, eyes closed.

Andrew now began to feel a tingling sensation. His fear of the public was gone. Something inside his blood started to creep up from toes and fingers, up legs and arms, a sensation moving towards the groin. Sexual arousal.

Andrew looked around and saw people shifting in their seats, blushing, trying to calm their breathing, the men hiding their groins. Nora had a look of shocked disapproval on her blushing face. David had a hard-on pushing through his underwear. The feeling slowly went away, and so did David's visible erection, up there, on stage.

A sense of calm began to set in, followed by a crawling melancholia. A rush of tears filled up David's face and the eyes of most people in the audience. Then it turned to rage as David opened his eyes again and stared straight at Harvey and Nora, who also looked back, enraged, with similar looking eyes.

David, sitting in his chair on the stage, burst out laughing, and so did everyone else. These ups and downs continued, until a middle-aged man in the crowd clutched his left arm, then his chest, and yelled 'medic!' Then a woman also asked for a doctor, ripped her wires out and stumbled off, followed by half of the enraged audience, including Harvey and Nora, while Andrew and the remaining crowd stood up and began to clap, slowly at first, then louder and faster and then they cheered, as David also clapped and cheered, and everyone kept crying with happiness, yelling, along with David: 'Bravo! Bravo!'

The Shoes

'Hi, HOW ARE YOU, BOOBOOCHOPS?'

'Yes, all good, how are things at the money-making machine?' That's what Lavinia called Philippe's financial firm.

'Busy.'

'Still, you find the time to call…'

'Hearing your voice gives me a motivational boost, you know it.'

'Glad to be of service.'

'I don't mean it that way.'

'I know, it's just that I'm busy preparing for dinner.'

'Christopher is coming.'

'Francesca is really nervous about his first dinner with us. It is her first time she brings a boyfriend to dinner, after all.'

'But we've known him for weeks now.'

'Never had dinner at the house, though.'

'It'll be fine.'

Normally the evening would start with the chatter and tales of school gossip and office battles, the epic description of a faraway world of conflicts and confrontations, so distant from Lavinia's smooth, rhythmic, easy-listening life. While

Philippe had been in finance since getting out of college, she had never been interested in making money but was elated to share the lifestyle. She never had the ambition to leave Islington and move to a brownstone near Holland Park. Quite a move up. But now, the spacious studio gave her a chance to nurture her acrylic painting, then move to oil and collage with mixed techniques. She was not that dedicated. She spent most of the day with the difficult task of doing nothing. The girls were in school most of the day; helpers made dinner and cleaned up, entering and leaving with little noise. Soft country music on Spotify in the background erased the sense of time passing, and it was dinnertime before she could realize it.

She was rearranging the furniture, after having moved a painting to a different wall, when Francesca charged in, as usual.

'How was school?'

'Who cares, really? Christopher will be here any minute.'

'I know, but no reason to not have a proper conversation while preparing for the arrival of your …? What do we call him?'

'Love-slash-friend?'

Slash. The slash generation, Lavinia thought. The constant indecisions and ambiguity. Good-slash-bad. Whatever.

'Just that, slash-friend?'

'Yeah, no, you are right. He's my…'

'Boo, bae, beau?' Lavinia had googled politically correct ways to say, boyfriend. 'Er … manfriend? Your … guy? No, wait … significant other?'

'Partner.'

'Doesn't that also mean spouse? I know that at eighteen you can use adult definitions, but still … is it accurate?'

'It's fine, a partner is not a spouse, is it?'

'You are both mature enough to define each other as you see fit and all the rest...'

Francesca looked up at her, a quick glance, then continued setting up the table.

The dinner went smoothly. Christopher fit in easily. Not too aggressive, not too appeasing with Francesca's younger sister either, encapsulating himself in the family by making the occasional right observation, adding the prompt suggestion at the correct moment. They loved how it felt like he belonged. The partner…

'A mature boy for our mature daughter,' Philippe said to Lavinia, later, in bed.

'But shouldn't Francesca have asked us if he could sleep over?' Lavinia said, rolling her eyes towards the wall, in the direction of their daughter's room.

Philippe didn't answer. They both lay there in bed, staring at the ceiling.

'Did we do the right thing?' Philippe said.

Now it was Lavinia who didn't answer. It seemed that they were trying to hear if there was a sound coming from beyond the thin walls of their Holland Park home.

'Do you want to…?' Lavinia said, kissing Philippe on the cheeks, caressing his hip and moving her hand down his leg.

'Feels weird.'

'Yes, you are right…Me too.'

'Why?'

'Them?'

'Yeah…'

The morning after, Lavinia, who normally liked to get up after everybody else, surprisingly walked Philippe to the front door and kissed him goodbye. As he walked out in the hall, he stumbled on something on the floor. He looked down, and with a nervous kick he swept aside what had made him trip, then made for the door.

Lavinia leaned down in the semi-obscurity of the hallway, searching for what had made Philippe stumble. It was a pair of shoes. A man's shoes. But they were not Philippe's. They were Christopher's bulky loafers.

Holding one in her hand, Lavinia sat down on the floor and while looking at it she began to weep silently.

Single-sheet Paper Holder

SEAN IS STILL UPSTAIRS. PATRICK KEEPS CHECKING THE building's door to see when his friend will open it. Sean always keeps his friend waiting in the car.

Patrick will text him laconic: 'Here.'

Sean will text back: 'Coming.'

And then it will take him another ten minutes for Sean to get downstairs.

'Everything okay?' Patrick says once Sean sits in the passenger seat and buckles up, bringing into the car a mix of a pleasant aftershave and a slight halitosis.

'Yeah, all good. I was on the phone with Clara and when I get to the elevator the signal gets cut off, so I had to finish my conversation before coming down.'

'Sure, no problem,' Patrick says and takes off a bit too abruptly, considering his smooth driving style.

'She's not happy with me.'

'Who?' asked Patrick.

'Clara. We're kind of back together now, after I made her move out when I had … well, you remember. She's volunteering in a dog shelter now.'

'That's good, she's a natural when it comes to caregiving.'

'She is. Look, I don't care about any of that. What if she wants to play mother with me? It's fine.'

'I didn't mean that.'

'She says I need a job. Like, a real one, not the freelance stuff I do from home. I need an office, a school where I can teach. I tried. It's not easy, never lasts, doesn't help. Then I come home, collapse on the kitchen floor, eyes closed, can't move. I'm on the third shrink in two years. Keep saying to myself I shouldn't feel guilty about not having a job and feeling like a constant failure since I achieved nothing in life.'

'We all feel like that. But the rest of us doesn't care. You do. That's the difference. No more lithium?'

'No more chemicals, they drive you mad.'

Patrick and Sean were so engrossed in the conversation they had barely noticed the blood sky of the lurid sunset surrounding them. Plunged in their own words, as if those conversations could bring them out of this feeling of sinking in a maelstrom.

'I always feel like I should be getting you out of these ruts. But it's not working. Not any longer.'

'You remember the best friend I had before meeting you?' Sean asked. 'The one who died of cancer.'

'Yes.'

'Last time I saw him he gave me something. A totally pointless object, I thought. But, whatever, it's what he left me, so I have cherished it for so long. What mattered was not what it was for but that he gave it to me. It could have been anything.'

They were back on Patrick's street, now, after the long, aimless drive which they took just to be together, to catch up while sheltering from the cold.

'Sorry about what I said earlier. I am grateful for your help, always. Even twenty years ago when I was about to … you remember. But nothing has changed with me. I have recently realized I've always been like this.'

Sean pulled something out of his pocket and handed it to Patrick. It was a strange, round plastic thing with a flat base. It looked like it had a cut right across it. Sean thought it looked like the chopped snout of a sand-coloured Kermit the Frog. It had a bureaucratic beige hue.

'It's a single-sheet paper holder. You can slide a single sheet in it when you are trying to transcribe something or if you're playing music. It will make the sheet stand straight up. It's a silly thing but…' Sean broke out crying. Patrick was puzzled.

'Take it. It was given to me, now I give it to you.'

'What are you saying? Don't do this…' Patrick said.

'Just take it, please.'

Speechless, Patrick held the strange paper holder in his hand. It was heavy, probably made of iron and covered in plastic, he thought. Sean hugged Patrick, crossing over the stick shift and handbrake, and squeezed hard in a tight grip of desperation. Then, as Sean was sobbing, unexpectedly, he kissed Patrick's cheek, something that had never happened before.

Speechless, Patrick held the strange little paper holder in his hands. Sean opened the door and disappeared into his building.

As Patrick was driving towards his home, he was puzzled but also drained. He felt he had done enough saving of Sean's life. Enough. It was too much. And plus, it didn't seem to work.

Three weeks went by. He did not hear from Sean. He was always afraid he might get a call from Clara or from Sean's mom announcing his friend had ended it. Patrick called him. 'I don't have enough strength to even talk now, forgive me,' Sean said and hung up.

He called back two weeks later. Sean's tone, over the phone, seemed less morose. He was trying to go for walks, he said. The therapy seemed to be working. The clinical diagnosis was clear. He was relieved.

The time came to go for another drive. They decided that this time Sean would pick up Patrick. Quite unusual. 'Your driver is here, sir,' the text message said. Sean was smiling when Patrick got in the car.

'I am having a season of relative stability.'

'Did you get on the meds?'

'None of that.'

'How, then?'

'I've understood something. I thought about you and Clara and how all of you, who are normal, are able to do it, how you manage to stay alive, to delude yourself that this thing, this life, has any meaning. The secret is to pretend you are a saviour, not a victim. You don't even need to become one. Just pretend. It's all about how you tell yourself who you are. The problem with me is I can't bullshit myself well enough. Act your part. That's the secret.'

'Realizing you can try to help other people made you want to live? But you've always been generous as a friend, a partner to Clara, you are not self-centred at all.'

'It's not about what it is, it's what you think of it.'

'But did you just wake up one day and realize this?'

'Something happened. Clara hurt her foot. She had to have surgery. She still can't move. She can't come over to the house and have dinner with me, can't drive to work, can't be my nurse, my caring mother figure she likes so much to be. She's now like me, in a way. A victim. Stuck. Her immobility has given me a chance to make myself feel indispensable. Her broken foot has cured me!' Sean smiled, then he laughed out loud.

Suddenly, Patrick felt sad. He should've been happy for his friend's recovery. For the fact he not only did not kill himself but was finally in good spirits, driving, joking, laughing.

Something was wrong, Patrick thought. Was it the beginning of his own depression?

He thought it was not yet time to return the single-sheet paper holder to Sean. He would just hold on to it a bit longer. You never know. It made him feel good to have it.

The Umbrella

We hope people who love them will find comfort in visiting their profile to remember and celebrate their life.

Learn more about the legacy contact setting and memorialized accounts on Facebook.

The most recent posts in her timeline say:

'Trust the process,' and

'Every next level of your life
will demand a different you.'

Photos of book covers lying on an elegant coffee table.

The Flowers of Evil, by Charles Baudelaire and the lessons of Krishnamurti.

A quote:

There are no facts
only interpretations
Friedrich Nietzsche.

Posted on 15 December 2015

The caption to a photograph of a sign in a building complex called 'JASMINE'

'My new and very first home on my
own in a building named Jasmine.
one of the happiest moments
of my life. Feeling blessed… 😊
#home #jasmine'

Posts on Smell Dating.

Cute cats snapshots.
'Home is where your cat is… 😊
back home to these beauties. Happiness'

Then another quote, by photographer William Albert Allard.

'As we all know, when something terrible
happens to someone we
love, it can be heart-breaking. And
there seem to be no words to truly
express the feeling of such hurt.'

The last post is on 1 October 2016. Four days before it happened.

* * *

I remember the last time we met. I remember the first time we met.

She was travelling a lot at the time, living a sort of Renaissance, after her divorce. Venice, Berlin, Paris, Istanbul, Rome, Florence, London, Mumbai. She'd post newspaper clippings of interviews and profiles that national newspapers and magazines were beginning to print about her.

Petite, well-shaped, radiant, velvety gaze, and blissful smile. Sexy, undoubtedly. Almost always dressed in flowing white skirts or dresses that enhanced the smoothness of her brown skin and gave her an air of spirituality. A message to the world that said, 'I've done yoga and meditation'.

The first time we met, she asked if she could lean closer to smell my neck. There was nothing untoward. But it was a sort of handshake, a way to see if we could get along. She seemed pleased. We could be friends. Her capacity to consolidate a fraternal bond was so fast that I found myself writing to friends in Milan and Rome that they had to meet her when she came to visit. My sister was expecting her in Los Angeles when she would go on her next business trip. Although she never made it there.

The last time I saw her, we were sitting by a pool, at the Vivenda dos Palhaços hotel de charme in Goa. I listened to her in total enchantment of the intellectual and artistic brilliance of her project.

'What is your favourite period in history?' she asked.

'I don't know, hard to tell, but I have a few.'

'Okay, so which era of the past would you like to have lived in, let's put it that way…' she insisted

'I like the fifties, maybe because that's when my mother was a teenager, and she still has a fifties vibrancy about her. And the twenties, when things seemed so promising, before political and economic disaster hit the world … and perhaps the last twenty-five years of the 1800s, all those inventions and plans to change the world, which worked, although not necessarily for the better … then the mid-1500s in Italy, so much talent, and the weirdness of Ancient Rome, but I'd have to have been a patrician, definitely not into the slave/gladiator business!'

'Okay, so what I'm doing now is trying to capture the scent, the perfume, the essence of the smell of eras. I began with the seventies, fifties, thirties and then 1880 and 1776. Here, these are the bottles.' She opened a little leather case and extracted miniature tester vials the colour of amber, gold and rust. A heady and dreamy aroma filled the air.

'Show me your wrist,' she said as she suddenly sprayed a misty cloud of fragrance on my skin.

'Now, tell me, which year are we in?'

'Hmm, tobacco, leather, these are manly times. Perhaps the thirties?'

'You're right! Brilliant.'

'And now…?' She sprayed another bottle on the other wrist.

'Something exotic, but also slightly aggressive, citrusy, but also a scent of … a distant flavour of something slightly bitter, maybe patchouli. I'd guess we're in the seventies?'

'Yes, you got it, perfect!' her eyes were squinting with joy but letting through a piercing gleam, a probing gaze that didn't let you off the hook. A lot of willpower and determination, fierce desire to emancipate, conquer, seduce, build and grow was reflected in her movements and tone of voice.

She gave me a little vial filled with a refreshing jasmine scent. 'It's going to smell good on you, it's a good combination for your natural scent, try it.' I still have it.

We chatted on Facebook, mostly me giving advice for her travels, looping her with my friends scattered around the world, friends who I thought would be enchanted to meet someone like her.

I went back to read what we said, in those months in 2015. She was always 'absolutely looking forward' to her next journey to Europe. Or 'excited to say the least' and 'wishing an amazing year ahead'. The simple and kind enthusiasm of a Millennial who wants to project a positive outlook, an optimistic charm. Biagio and Annamaria, the dear friends I introduced her to, were 'absolute gems. Without them, Milan would have been so different and cold. They looked after me like a princess … So much love and warmth.' Then she was trying to find a place to stay in Venice, for the Biennale. I couldn't help her, but 'something will eventually turn up,' she wrote me, and it did. Everyone wanted to contribute to make her great, to help her in this battle, which was the battle of a young single Indian woman who was building herself up as an entrepreneur, a businessperson with a unique gift, that of being 'a nose', someone capable of discerning specific smells, but also of creating good combinations. 'Independent perfume research and designer', the newspapers said when profiling her ascent. Some claimed that perhaps she was the only one in India adopting the European perfume tradition and techniques.

She was going to make it. She was making it. She was determined to become a symbol. She felt she already was. She was going to have the success she felt she deserved. Perhaps even more success now that she walked away from the protective yet sometimes overpowering presence of a talented husband. Everyone rooted for her. She was now living by herself, in an elegantly furnished three-bedroom flat in a big, cosmopolitan and coastal city of India.

That day, on those wooden chairs, on those soft cushions by the swimming pool, with the ageing Basset Hound Gigolo swinging his long soft ears as he crossed the well-tended lawn, she suddenly asked to see the lines on my palm. I had always thought that her voluminous mane of shiny curly hair gave her the air of a gentle sorceress.

'It's all noticeably clear. Here is the lifeline. It splits twice. Once at sixteen. Here, you see, this is the parallel life you would've had if you had continued on your course, at that age. It wouldn't have lasted long. You saved yourself at that age.'

'I left home,' I said. 'I moved to another continent altogether and never went back to my family…'

'And here's the other positive but very deep change. It's recent. This must be when you met your wife…' I looked over at my wife, who was swimming in the pool as we chatted. We were there to celebrate her birthday with a dozen good friends, that day of December.

'And what does your lifeline say?' I asked.

'I will die at thirty-nine.'

* * *

The Flowers of Evil.

Scroll…

A new home in a building called Jasmine, her favourite fragrance.

Scroll…

When something terrible happens to someone you love; it can be heart-breaking.

Death was coming for her. And she did know when.

The rest is news reports.

12 October 2016

PANAJI – A security guard has confessed he hid for two days on the terrace of perfumer Monika Ghurde's apartment complex before breaking into her home, sexually abusing and killing her, the Goa Police said on Tuesday.

Ms Ghurde, 39, was found dead, tied to her bed in Goa's Sangolda Village on 5 October. Three days later, 21-year-old Rajkumar Singh, a security guard at the complex, was arrested in Bengaluru where he was caught using Ms Ghurde's ATM card. Singh has admitted he had been obsessed with the perfumer since the day she came looking for an apartment.

'It was around 6.35 p.m. when I went to her flat and knocked on the door as the bell was not functioning,' Singh confessed, 'she shouted "kaun?" (who is it?) and I said I was the company supervisor. Had I told her I was the security guard, she would not have opened the door. When she did, I showed her the knife I was holding. I told her not to shout. But she screamed loudly, so I gagged her mouth for nearly five minutes then she fell unconscious. I dragged her to the bedroom and put her on the bed. I asked her why she had complained against me, but she denied it. I told her that I had been thrown on the road. I lost my job, my money and my two bags too. All this happened on the day I was to get my salary. They did not pay me any money. She tried to change my mind, offered me mango chocolates. She said she would give me a job; she would keep me as her personal driver and bodyguard. I said that anyone in her position would say these things. And then she said she would give me her bank cards. But I didn't know how to use them. I asked if she had enough money in the account. She explained to me how to put in the card, select the language and withdraw. I thought I would tie her up and step out to try to use the cards. But I was confused. If I let go of her, she would complain, and I would be in a complete mess. I didn't know what to do. A few hours passed. I cooked some eggs, shaved, took a shower, and put on her brother's clothes. This is when I forced myself on her and took a video of it on my phone. I thought I would blackmail her. If she complained to the police, I would post it on YouTube, I said. I told her that I had come only for the money, not to kill her. If I wanted to kill her, I would have done it five hours before. I put the knife on the floor and was releasing her when she picked it up. I threw it aside and smothered her. I thought she had fainted. I tied her hands back on the bed and walked out of the flat. I went to the beach and at 11 in the morning went to the railway station. I wanted to go up to Chandigarh or Amritsar, but there was a train to Mangaluru. That's how I reached Bengaluru. I bought a SIM card from a beggar with 1000 rupees to check with the other security personnel to see what happened. That's when the police caught me.'

During the interrogation, Singh admitted the crime was prompted by his anger of losing his job after Ms Ghurde accused him of stealing an umbrella. The umbrella was found on Singh at the moment of the arrest.

The Candy Box

'I USED TO BE FAT. VERY FAT. AN OSTENTATIOUSLY FAT BOY. Fattest boy in my class. A health problem, really. Being that fat. Look, I still have a photo … let me get it. See? Fat. Long hair to try to make my fat face less round. *Chubby Cheekers*, they called me. Fatness made me sad. Isolated. I had to build a world of my own. When I was twelve, it got to be so painful, being singled out as the fattest boy in the room, that I decided to do something about it. Started to play badminton. More and more seriously. After months of obsessive badminton, I began to lose weight. Over the years, I gained muscles, toned arms, legs, stomach. Eating healthy. I became unbearable, proselytizing to everyone about the nourishing benefits of fresh juice and badminton. No booze. It wasn't easy because, you know, this town, here, where my mother lives now, has the highest alcoholism rate in the county, which is the county with the highest alcoholism rate in Wales so…'

'So, your mother is the most alcoholic in the town of the most alcoholic county in Wales?' the guy interrupted him with a stupid grin.

Shirish fell silent. For a second, he considered smacking this young man he had just met in the pub, who thought it was appropriate to make fun of his mother. Then he remembered the violent boy hidden within him – the irate fat kid who wanted to smack this semi-stranger was not really him. The new him, who had emerged when he was twelve, had learned to take things with humour.

'I w-w-wish,' he stuttered. Then, calmly, 'my mother drinks half a glass only on special occasions. No, no drinking. She has other addictions. Like shopping for useless things. When she goes out, she always comes back with something that has no purpose. The house is filled with souvenirs, little statuettes, miniature dolls. A whole world of pointlessness. It's as if she is trying to fill a void. There's always room for more. Can't control it. But when it comes to drinking … it's not in her tradition and she's perfectly capable of keeping those urges in check. It's mine she feeds…'

'What do you mean?' the guy asked.

'When I visit her, like I have to, later today, she has a special treat for me.'

'That's sweet.'

'Exactly the point. I shouldn't have sweets.'

'No, I meant …'

'I know what you meant.'

'You seem fit, man, what are you complaining about?'

'I am forced to stay fit; don't you get it? I burst out like an airbag if I don't work out once a day and if I don't watch what I eat.'

'Damn...'

'Very quick. Also, I must exercise to keep this,' Shirish said pointing to his torso, 'if I let go, I swell up and go back from this,' He pointed again to himself, 'to … that!' Shirish indicated the round-cheeked boy in the photo on his phone

–Shirish as a long-haired boy, many eons and kilos ago. The boy in the photo has a hint of a smile, but his eyes are melancholic.

'That's how I was able to turn my life around. What made me become an independent businessman in my twenties. Escaping my fate as an overweight boy … I discovered a secret of life, a tiny switch of how you change things …'

Time to change the subject, Shirish thought, as he flashed his famous extra-wide smile. The guy he had just met at the pub noticed his full mouth with sensual lips opening to slightly irregular, brightly white teeth flashing a charming grin. The choppers looked like they had rushed to the mouth all at the same time, in a hurry to fill that needy mouth, as if those teeth had no time to settle properly in a row.

Probably had one too many drinks, Shirish thought. Rambling. Revealing too much. Not in control. Too extroverted. *I'm too hungry and too sociable.*

'I feel like I'm one of those people truly without a homeland. I mean, my family came from Karnataka, originally.'

'Sounds like martial arts. Where is it, Indonesia?'

'India. See, there you go … To people like you, who feel like you've belonged here for generations, I'll always be a foreigner because I come from a family of foreigners. I was born and raised here, just like you. India is unknown to me. Never been there. Don't feel the need to go. Noise, food too spicy, communicable diseases, and what about the traffic? Maybe that's what I am missing, that feeling of a place where…'

'Maybe that's why you're stuffing yourself like that,' the guy said, noticing how Shirish was plunging handfuls of peanuts and crisps into his mouth, drifting back to his uncontrollable appetite.

'Maybe,' Shirish said, 'although I really try to avoid cheap psychological interpretations, Doctor Freud. Anyway, got to go, it's teatime and Mam's waiting.'

Shirish paid and left, wobbling down the street to his mother's house. Houses and cars seemed blurred in his peripheral vision at first, but as he walked his mind cleared a bit.

As usual, his mother was alone in the living room. Droning noise from the screen. He still felt tipsy; hues appeared softened, sounds louder. All those little objects, dolls, souvenirs seemed to stare at him, waiting for him to do or say something.

'Please turn that off, Mam,' Shirish slurred.

His mother smiled at him, got out of her armchair, and scuttled to the kitchen.

'Come, Shirish!' she called out to him.

His gaze turned sad. He sighed and joined her at the kitchen table. Kettle bubbling, teacups clanking. He despised being there, and at the same time felt protected and nestled.

Then he saw her do what he always dreaded. She opened the cupboard. Reached inside to get something. Out came the candy box. A metallic colourful little square. From India. He asked himself if parents ever realize that what they transform their children into does not always correspond to what their children want to be.

'Come on, Shirish, you are being too hard on yourself. Have one. Please. Just one,' his mother said as she set the box down on the table.

'What the hell, Mam, what did I tell you about bringing out sweets when I visit! Why are you still doing this to me! How many times do I have to tell you to please work with me, not against me! You're unbearable when you do this! Why?'

Shirish sighed. Scowled. His well-toned shoulders slumped. His mother sat there, on the other side of the table with an expression that said very clearly: let him vent it out. It was an almost indifferent gaze, but underneath it there was an imperceptible smile, the two ends of her lips curling up ever so slightly. It was Saraswathi, Lakshmi, Parvati, Kali, all crunched into a single, strong-willed, intense, warm, and soft Mother who just wanted him to lie down with his head on her lap so she could caress his hair, as she did when he was a child.

Then, she lifted the lid off the candy box as she looked at Shirish with a stronger hint of that loving smile. Shirish waited for a bit, frowning. He sighed and felt sad, like in that old, black-and-white picture on his phone. Something woke up inside him. A feeling that began near his belly button and inched up his sternum into his chest and slowly into his throat, up through the esophagus, finally liquefying into his palate, as his tongue felt wet, and he swished some saliva between his teeth and his tongue. He swallowed and felt his mouth drying again.

He slowly reached for the box to pluck out and push into his irregularly toothed mouth the first of many sweets.

The Wind-up Cockroach

'Come in!' Mark yelled from the couch where he was leafing through a magazine while Lydia was busy answering emails. Someone kept knocking nervously at the door upstairs. They were renting a basement in Williamsburg for the summer with a four-poster bed, vintage sofas, country-style wooden tables and a floor-to-ceiling window. The apartment faced a small courtyard, which climbed to a green garden with cherry trees and rose bushes. There were two doors at the top of the stairs. One led to a street in Brooklyn, the other to the owner's apartment, where the knocking came from.

'I'm showing the basement to a possible tenant, you guys, is that okay?' the owner, Patricia, who preferred to be called Trish, announced loudly as she opened the door.

Mark and Lydia heard steps slowly descending the glass-bottom staircase. It was a beautiful and peculiar set of transparent steps that allowed a wide skylight to brighten the basement. The stairs ended in front of a deformed mirror and, below, in a large glass square box that contained a three-foot-wide clock – an unequivocal homage to Alice in Wonderland.

Mark noticed the slow steps descending the stairs, high heels hitting the glass panes with unhurried rhythm. It was certainly not Trish, who always seemed in a rush and rarely wore formal shoes. The possible tenant, Mark thought. He noticed the first shoe, black, matte, pointy, elegant, followed by a proportionate ankle which continued in a toned calf. Then another step and a stylish dark skirt appeared, partly covered by the power jacket of a woman who wants to communicate to the world that not only is she in business, but she knows her business. A strong hand was now holding the rail like a queen holding a sceptre. Long, thin black hair, a rebel bang falling on her forehead. She brushed it aside, puffing air from her full lips. The woman had an ancient Roman's nose, which some would call a Greek profile. It was her most prominent feature, supported by a strong enough jaw. When she turned her dark eyes to the basement and her mouth opened in a captivating smile, Mark's heart began to pump a little faster, his breath cut short, and a slight perspiration formed around his hairline.

It was Angela. She now recognized him too, but neither of them said anything. As she descended, Mark noticed she was holding an arm up in the air, towards the top of the stairs, perhaps holding someone's small hand. He had to control himself and to think of a strategy. And fast. Would they pretend not to know each other? Would he introduce Angela to Lydia? Or would they make believe they were just distant acquaintances who had met each other once or twice somewhere else?

Mark had met Angela seven years earlier under curious circumstances. They were both spending New Year's Eve in the same expensive Keralan Ayurvedic clinic, undergoing

Panchakarma cures to expunge from their metabolism the respective consorts they had recently been divorced from. Mark at the time was a failed middle-aged novelist who still insisted on trying to write while slowly extinguishing the savings accumulated in his youth as a well-paid advertising copywriter. Angela was a successful literary agent who needed a break from the Manhattan rat race and had a lot of great leads from her bestselling Indian authors on what to visit in Kerala.

They had run into each other at the swimming pool, where they began to bond as adoptive New Yorkers and as literati. After an uneventful New Year's Eve party, gazing at the fireworks lighting up the south Indian sky over the ocean, having established a total absence of any sexual spark between them, they decided to continue their journey together through southern India. Strictly as friends. They had both wanted to explore what he explained, while pedantically reading aloud from a tourist guide, were the biggest backwaters in the world.

This is how, after a loud and colourful ride in a stylish vintage white Ambassador car, they found themselves on a two-night cruise aboard a riverboat, complete with a crew, captain, sailor and cook. They had sternly insisted with the agency upon having a two-cabin boat. They were nothing more than newly met friends, with no intentions of sharing the same bed, Angela explained. The boat rental agent insisted there were no boats available with two cabins, only with one. He also explained how much they could save by renting a boat with just one cabin. The two-cabin boat was truly excessive considering there were only two passengers, he kept repeating. It seemed apparent to him that Angela and Mark were a good match, although they might not have known it then.

But Angela knew how to get her way. She was one of the best New York literary agents, after all. She told everyone she was from Rome, but, in fact, she hailed from Morlupo, a small town on the ancient Flaminia way, along the last dozens of kilometres the Roman armies had to march through before returning to the Eternal City.

She kept her humble roots a secret for most of her life and from most people. She had not confessed to anyone, not even her aristocratic first husband, about her Morlupo bond. The name's etymology was tricky. Some historians believed it meant the Mountain of the Wolf, others that it evoked a wolf's death. Mor Lupo. Die Wolf! The most believable hypothesis, however, revealed that this village was an ancient colony of Roman soldiers called Martis Rapaces Lupi, the rapacious wolves of the God of War, Mars. Mark had looked all that up, after the trip … The town was built by roughnecks, highway robbers, exiled soldiers of ancient empires, banished outside the city walls, but close enough to reap from its riches. This is the spirit she evoked in herself when she needed to get into combat mode, just as now when she needed a two-cabin boat for the Keralan backwaters cruise.

Begging, smiling, getting irritated, assertive, then flexible and reasonable, interrogating, asking questions, bribing. She won. And they sailed off in the late afternoon, welcomed by the sweetest golden sunset they could wish for, hoping it would drown the famous lingering melancholy of being recently divorced. After a fulfilling seafood dinner on the boat, they retired to their separate cabins.

Mark was woken up in the middle of the night by loud rapping on his cabin door. Are we sinking? was his first thought. Then he heard Angela's voice repeating his name, dragging on the 'a' of Mark with that intriguing Italian accent. Mahrk ... She was quite agitated and asked him to follow her to her cabin.

'Angela...' Mark said, raising his eyebrows as far away from his eyes as he could and tilting his head, to give her a scolding look.

'No, no, it's not what you think. Here, come, see for yourself!' She pointed to the cupboard of her cabin, where Mark immediately spotted a large, brownish, long-antennaed disgusting cockroach slowly inching up the side of the door.

'I can take anything but not cockroaches, sorry, Mahrk,' she concluded.

'What do we do?' Mark asked.

'I mean, if you don't mind, maybe we could switch cabins...' she said.

Mark sighed. 'I'm sorry, really sorry, but I confess that I am just as disgusted by cockroaches as you are, and I wouldn't be able to sleep here either.'

They went back to Mark's cabin and inspected his cupboard to determine there were no insects there. So, they resolved to do what the rental agent and common sense had suggested all along – they shared the same bed.

Mark resisted for a little while, in the silence of that floating boat, anchored in some distant dock off the backwater's coastline. Angela had tossed and turned at the appropriate moment, signalling she was not able to sleep either.

His hand reached for her fingers. It could be something that happened by mistake. But he left the hand there, above hers. She did not pull away. Slow caresses started to signal the beginning of an affair about which they would grow different expectations.

Angela was still recovering from a divorce which had been a setback on many levels. She had arrived in the States as a student of Contemporary Literature at New York University. After her Master of Arts, she had gotten an internship at the office of the fiercest and most respected literary agency in New York.

Her new boss seemed to embody everything Angela did not want to become but ended up becoming within ten years. The woman was relentless, apparently jovial, eternally glacial and calculating, always thinking about a work opportunity, on the lookout for a connection, a deal. Fiercely unforgiving, exploitative, and rude to those below her.

Angela was better looking than her boss. Her Mediterranean sensuality was a useful tool in her climb up the slippery power ladder from intern to junior partner. Her eyes always seemed to hint at a possibility, corroborated by her Sophia Loren pout, which often turned into a quick, quizzical smirk. It was no surprise to all her friends that she soon found herself married to a soft-willed, decadent young Roman count from Papal nobility, living in a high rise overlooking the East River. As the Contessa of the Upper East Side, she was now on her way to conquer better and better positions in New York's publishing and literary world.

Unfortunately, her husband felt too crushed by the strong will of this Contessa di Morlupo once he found his way into the arms of an accommodating post-graduate assistant from Greenwich, Connecticut, with whom he soon fathered an heir to the dynasty.

This unleashed an inebriating season of sexual freedom for Angela but also professional and personal freedom. She was finally able to bring to her newly furnished, well-appointed one-bedroom in Central Park West some of the aspiring, handsome and energetic writers who wanted to be represented by her now independent agency. This is when Mark had stepped into her life, in Kerala.

Their affair had lasted a few months, with meetings in London, New York, Rome – an exalting passion which soon fizzled out, at least for the unreliable Mark, who was already in bed with another woman in a Soho loft while, in an Upper East Side antique shop, Angela was buying a most curious memento: a rusty wind-up made-in-Japan metallic toy, a replica of a giant cockroach. It skidded on the floor for a few seconds, as the spring mechanism was released.

The most peculiar thing that Mark would remember about Angela, and which immediately flashed in his mind when he saw her descending those stairs in Williamsburg, was that she had a fetish Mark had read and heard about but had never had the chance to experience first-hand. This was something that Angela liked to do, evidently.

As they were in bed in the Cinnamon Suite of the Malabar Hotel in Fort Kochi, making love for the third or fourth time after the backwaters cruise, Angela kissed him on the mouth, then descended on his nipples, his belly, groin, sex and, which is what surprised Mark, did not stop but continued down his thighs, knees (when will she stop, Mark asked himself now), on to the shins, ankles, feet and she finally reached his rather round and not particularly appealing right toe and began to slowly suck it for a very long time, as in a perfect fellatio. Mark felt uneasy at first, yet excited as well, and coming to realize three things. First of all, that this was the kind of thing that the person doing it would enjoy more than the person receiving it. Secondly, that he wasn't sure he wanted to kiss her after all the toe-sucking. And, thirdly, it felt odd that someone so squeamish about an insect pest would not be disgusted at all about licking and sucking such parts of a human body.

Whenever he looked at the wind-up cockroach she had gifted him, he couldn't help associating it with the toe-sucking. Which, when he thought about it, was the reason their love story did not work.

In the following years, once they'd broken off all communication, Mark had wanted to mail back her rusted ornament but never did. He kept it as a memento of a good, short relationship that had turned sour. But also, a memento of another secret which was in danger of being finally eviscerated.

The end of the relationship had been Mark's fault. He simply started being slower at answering messages and returning calls, having other things to do, making himself unavailable in that cowardly way that some men can still think they can get away with. He was not yet aware of what the word 'ghosting' meant. She eventually relented; understood he was phasing her out. And never contacted him again.

Only years later, when Mark ran into a common acquaintance, did he realize Angela had been mortally offended by this lame way of separating. Never mind, he thought, another disgruntled, bitter ex-lover in a list of haters that, as Mark aged, increased slowly but steadily.

Mark didn't want to admit why he did not want to tell his wife Lydia about having met Angela before, as Angela was stepping into their rented basement in Williamsburg. Too much emotional baggage in the way the relationship ended, Mark thought. But the real reason was walking down the steps holding Angela's hand.

It was a ridiculously small hand, Mark noticed. A child's hand. A girl. The girl. That girl, Mark thought, remembering a common acquaintance who had told him that, shortly after their break-up, Angela had started a relationship with an English writer. On the rebound, as they say. Or was there something else behind her finding a boyfriend so soon after Mark phased out of their affair?

Angela had soon gotten pregnant, had separated from the English writer who did not want to be a father, and she decided to raise the child on her own. Mark had done the math and realized the last time he had slept with Angela could still be within the range of conception of this girl, who Mark had never seen before. But he had always chased away this thought, not wanting to find out if there was any truth in his repressed worry.

Angela took one more step and a pretty little blond girl appeared, smiling calmly, and staring intently at both Mark and Lydia.

'Hello,' Angela said.

'Hello,' said Lydia, who got up and went to greet the two visitors followed by Trish. Mark took an extra second getting up from the couch and stood there, waiting for them to get down and off the stairs. He looked at the girl, studying her features, his heart still uneasy and galloping in his chest.

He was afraid of recognizing something of himself in the little girl's face. At every step, a new detail of the beautiful girl's features was revealed in the light coming from the wide window, reflected on rows of well-watered plants.

Her straight little nose could not be inherited from her mother's Cleopatran one. Mark did indeed have a straight nose like that. The girl had dark, smiling eyes which Mark thought could or could not be like his. The shape of the jaw … perhaps, but hard to tell at that age. The blond hair had nothing to do with Mark's, except his father was blondish, so there could be a genetic strain. Mark tried to hide this torturous train of thought as much as possible, as the six-year-old finally reached the floor of the basement, smiling cordially at him.

'Hello,' Mark said to the girl. 'And what is your name?'

'Gioia.'

'Hello, Gioia. I'm Mark. How old are you, Gioia?'

Angela flashed a fierce look at Mark.

'I am six now.'

Mark immediately started to do some reverse calculations in his mind.

'Ah, six, you look so grown up to be only six. Good for you!' Mark said.

'Hello,' Mark said to Angela.

'Hi … I think we have met before, haven't we?' Angela said.

Mark looked at her. 'Oh, yes, of course, we met a few years ago, didn't we?'

'Yes, we did, a few years ago,' Angela said, looking around as if interested only in the apartment's decor.

'So, you're moving to Williamsburg,' Lydia interjected.

'Gioia's father is moving here, so I'd like her to be near him,' Angela said and began chatting with Lydia, while Mark tried to inconspicuously study Gioia's features.

He really could not tell if there was anything familiar in this little blond girl. Could he ever find out if this was his daughter? Did he want to? Was this Angela's revenge?

He never got an answer because soon Angela and Gioia were off, and Mark never met them again. They did not rent the basement apartment.

Acknowledgements

I WOULD LIKE TO ACKNOWLEDGE ALL THE ACQUAINTANCES, friends and relatives who might see something of themselves reflected through the prism of the stories in this collection. Some may be happy about it, some less so. Life is fleeting; we leave nothing behind and are soon forgotten. You might as well leave a story.

In my memoirs, novels (which I consider both as *memovels*, memoirs+novels), as well as in my short stories I have attempted to contemplate what is fictional within what is real, as I've tried to capture what is real in the fictional. Living can be experienced as a fictional story and reading a fictional story can be extremely close to a real-life experience.

Can this, perhaps, make life more fascinating, or more bearable?

Thanks

I want to thank Teo Pizzati for sharing his experiences during the pandemic lockdown in Rome in 2020, which provided some inspiration for 'The Mask'; The White House Farm Residency for hosting me in their cottage in Suffolk in 2018, which is the set for 'The smartphone'; and professor of philosophy Giorgio Agamben, for renting me his apartment in Paris in 2004, which inspired the setting for 'The Diaper'.

I also want to thank my wife, Tishani Doshi, for the valuable advice on this text, although she disagrees with some of my authorial choices.

About the Book

A candy box reveals a son's true feelings for his mother. A fish sculpture creeps into a budding and healthy relationship. A splint on a music teacher's finger threatens to expose a secret.

Objects can come to hold great power over life and the course it takes. This collection of short stories explores the nuances of the human experience as objects of sentimental value, nostalgic appeal or cultural significance bear witness and shed light on all that remains unsaid. *A History of Objects* expertly demonstrates the ways in which the inanimate are far from lifeless.

About the Author

Carlo Pizzati is the award-winning multilingual author of ten works of fiction and non-fiction in English and Italian. His most recent books are *La Tigre e il Drone* (2020), *Bending over Backwards* (2019) and *Mappillai* (2018). He contributes as a political analyst to the newspapers la *Repubblica* and la *Stampa.* He's based in Paramankeni, a fishermen's village in Tamil Nadu.